TEMPTED TO LOVE

In his long black trousers and white shirt the *Duc* looked, Ivona thought, very masculine, and at the same time very elegant. Even at a distance she felt the vibrations from him that made him different from any other man she had ever known. Love welled up inside her as if it was a flood tide she could not control.

It was a feeling she had never expected to experience and very different from anything she had anticipated. It was like a flame flickering in her body.

"I love him!" she whispered beneath her breath. "If he does not love me, at least I can see him, talk to him, be near him. . . ."

Tempted
to Love
Barbara Cartland

Tempted to Love

First Published in United States 1983
© 1983 Barbara Cartland
This Edition Published by **Book Essentials South** 1999
Distributed by **BMI**, Ivyland, PA 18974
PRINTED IN THE UNITED STATES OF AMERICA
ISBN 1-57723-422-7

Author's Note

The Franco-German war began on July 9, 1870. The defeat of the French Emperor and his Army at the battle of Sedan was disastrous.

The French were convinced that the reorganisation of their Armed Forces which had taken place after the Prussian defeat of Austria in 1866 made them the equal of the Germans. However, they had under Bismarck been preparing themselves for a long time, and their organisation, equipment, artillery and professional troops were far superior to the French.

Paris was bombarded and besieged but an Armistice was declared in January 1871.

The subsequent Peace Treaty was severe and kept France weak for years. Germany annexed Alsace and received a huge indemnity. Paris was not occupied, but suffered the Civic humiliation of a triumphant German march down the Champs Élysées.

In 1200, King Sverre of Norway sent out men on skis to reconnoitre before battle. In the Fifteenth, Sixteenth, and Seventeenth centuries skiing was used in warfare in

Finland, Norway, Poland, Russia and Sweden. From 1767 competitions were arranged for the ski troops.

Skiing as a sport really began in 1850 in Scandinavia and ten years later in California. The first big contest was held in Oslo in 1879 with ten thousand spectators and in the presence of the King. The Norwegians brought skiing to most countries by the end of the Nineteenth Century.

Chapter One
1870

"I have to die. . .I have to!" Ivona said to herself for the hundredth time.

The horses pulling the ancient and heavy carriage were moving slowly, and she knew it was because the snow driven on the wind was blinding the eyes of the animals.

But she was concerned only with wondering how she could kill herself and what would be the least painful way of doing it.

There was no alternative now; she had lain awake all night thinking what she should do, and today when the Nun came she knew she could not face the future and live.

It seemed impossible that her whole world had fallen into pieces so quickly and so unexpectedly.

She had been so happy with her mother in the *Comte*'s Château in the beautiful, mountainous country of Alsace, and she had thought when they got there four years ago that she would be safe.

Safe from the horror of her father's cruelty, the agony

on her mother's face, and the sound she would never forget of her mother screaming.

When they first arrived in France she had had nightmares night after night.

Then gradually, because they had been so happy and everything round them was so beautiful, she had begun to forget, until, like a streak of forked lightning, tragedy had struck.

She found it impossible to believe it true when they brought the two bodies, her mother's and the *Comte's*, back to the Château.

She had been roasting chestnuts over the fire for their return, knowing how they would laugh as they burnt their fingers.

At the same time, they would have enjoyed them, as they would enjoy the marshmallows which the Chef had made ready for her to toast in front of the big log fire.

A servant had come to the door to say:

"There's been an accident, *M'mselle!*"

She had gone out into the Hall to wait for the farm cart coming slowly down the drive, bringing in, covered in blankets, the bodies of the two people who had filled her whole world.

It was only after some of the *Comte's* family had arrived to take his body to his ancestral Château in the Loire to be interred in the family vault, and her mother had been buried in the small Churchyard in the village, that Ivona had faced her own future.

She had no idea what it would be, what she should do, or where she could go.

The *Comte's* relatives who had come to the Château were both gentlemen and they were kind and pleasant to her.

But it was obvious that they had no wish to be involved in their relative's private life, which was supposed to be kept secret from the rest of his family.

They were very polite, and the elder of them said to her:

"You can of course stay here, Lady Ivona, until you

have decided what you will do, and I expect that will be to return to England."

Because it was an idea that had never struck her, Ivona looked at him with startled eyes, and he went on quickly:

"Of course, if you need any money for travelling, or anything like that, you have only to ask me."

"Thank you, but I am quite all right."

She was, naturally, referring only to the fact that she had some money, although she had nothing else.

But now, when she thought about it, nothing was right, and the future seemed like a grey mist which she could not penetrate.

It was ominous that the *Comte's* relatives had addressed her by her own title, which she had never used all the time she was in France.

From the moment her mother and she ran away from the bleak, ugly grey house in Bedfordshire, her mother had reverted to her French nationality and used the name which had been hers before she married.

As the daughter of the *Comte* de Lesmont, Ambassador to the Court of St. James, she had been the loveliest débutante of the London Season, fêted and acclaimed by everybody who saw her.

Ivona had said to her once:

"As you were such a success, Mama, how could you have agreed to marry Papa?"

Her mother had sighed.

"It was not exactly a question of agreeing, dearest. Your father, as the Marquis of Morecombe, not only belonged to a distinguished and important family, he was also a very handsome man."

She sighed again as if she looked back into the past before she went on:

"When my father told me he had offered for me and he had agreed that we should be married, I thouht how very lucky I was, even though he was a good deal older than I was."

"But surely you would not have loved Papa?" Ivona insisted.

"I suppose I knew very little about love then," her mother answered. "I was flattered by his attention, and he was very different in the first years of our marriage from what he became. . .later."

When she thought of what had happened later, Ivona felt herself shrink and shiver, feeling as if some terrible darkness had fallen on her and her mother and never again would they see the sunlight.

It had all happened after the Marquis of Morecombe had had a bad fall from his horse out hunting.

He was an outstanding rider, and although he had fallen on his head and broken his collar-bone, they expected him to recover quickly and in a month or two to be his old self again.

He had always been a rather serious man, given to long silences when anything irritated or annoyed him, and he also had a temper which showed itself in icy, cutting remarks.

But usually, Ivona remembered, her mother could coax him into smiling again, and although everybody was a little afraid of "The Master's black moods," they were not very frequent.

Then after his accident everything was changed.

For months after his fall he would sit in a chair in his Study, taking no interest in his horses, his Estate, or his wife and daughter.

Then gradually, so gradually that it had not at first perturbed her, Ivona became aware that her father was becoming obsessively religious.

He introduced family prayers for the whole staff every morning, which he said had always been held in his father's time and his grandfather's before that.

He insisted on everybody attending two Services in the Church on the Estate every Sunday, and started Bible readings and prayers three times a week.

Anybody absent from these was severely reprimanded, and the readings, which gradually became more and more drawn out, began and ended with long prayers and were insufferably boring.

Although her mother had been a Catholic when she

married, her husband had forbidden her to attend her own Church and insisted that she accompany him to his.

Because she had always been sweet and pliable and wanted to make all those round her happy, her mother had obeyed her husband's command.

Only Ivona knew that she said her own Catholic prayers in the privacy of her bedroom and taught them to her daughter without her husband's knowledge.

When she was older, her mother had told her that she was a Catholic as all the de Lesmonts had been for generations, and when the Marquis was away from home she had taken her secretly to a Catholic Priest in the nearest town to have her baptised.

"It is wrong of me not to go to Mass as I should," she said to her daughter, "and to break with the traditions of my Church in letting you be brought up as a Protestant."

She sighed deeply before she went on:

"But while I want to please your father, I must try to save your soul, and if it has to be done secretly, I feel that God will forgive me."

By the time her mother had told her this, Ivona understood that many things had to be secret where her father was concerned.

Daily he seemed to grow more and more fanatically religious, and everything she did was wrong and irritated him.

The first time she realised what was happening to her mother, she was so shocked that for a week she felt sick and was unable to eat.

She might never have known what was occurring if her small spaniel dog, who was her inseparable companion, had not become ill in the night.

Ivona had put on her dressing-gown and slippers and taken him downstairs to let him out into the garden through the side-door.

Then as she waited for him she glanced up at her mother's bedroom window and saw that the light was on.

She feared that perhaps she had disturbed her mother and she would be wondering what was happening.

When the spaniel was ready to come in, she picked him up in her arms, locked the door, and went up the stairs.

Instead of going back to her own bedroom, she walked along the corridor to her mother's, thinking it would be best to explain what had happened so that her mother would not worry.

As soon as she reached the door she heard her mother saying:

"Please—George—please! You must not be so—cruel to me!"

She was sobbing, and her last words ended in a scream.

Incredibly, Ivona realised that her father was beating her mother. She heard the swish of a thin riding-whip, and each time it fell, her mother screamed and screamed again, until finally there were only groans, as if she had become semi-conscious.

Ivona stood paralysed at the door, unable to breathe, unable to understand.

Then she heard her father say heavily in a deep voice:

"I will pray for your soul, as I will pray for mine!"

As he spoke there was the sound of his heavy footsteps going across the room, followed by the sound of a door closing.

It was then, as if she came out of a trance, that Ivona put down the dog she was carrying and very tentatively opened the door of her mother's bedroom.

Her mother was lying on the floor, and for one terrifying moment she thought that she was dead.

She lay face-downwards, her hair spread over the carpet, and her thin nightgown was torn from her back and her skin was marked with a dozen weals from the whip, some of which were bleeding.

Afterwards Ivona could never bear to remember how she had helped her mother into bed, then held her close as she sobbed uncontrollably.

The tears had been running down her own face, and because her father had done such a terrible thing, some detached part of her mind was hating him and condemning him for his brutality.

When she looked back on that first horrifying revelation of what her mother was suffering, Ivona felt it was then that she had grown up.

She was no longer a child, but somebody facing problems that were too great and too frightening for her either to understand or to know how to solve.

After the same thing had occurred on two other occasions, Ivona realised that her mother was becoming a nervous wreck.

She had always been outstandingly beautiful, but now her eyes were sunken in her head, and there were deep dark lines under them which made her look very much older than she was.

She was always tense whenever her husband came into the room, and even when he was particularly pleasant she would tremble.

Because she thought her mother could not bear to talk of what was happening and was ashamed that her daughter should know what she was suffering, Ivona did not speak to her about it.

She was very intuitive where other people were concerned and extremely sensitive to their feelings.

She could understand that her mother felt humiliated that she should know she was being treated so brutally, and was in fact horrified that Ivona should have discovered by chance what was occurring.

The third time Ivona lifted her mother, unconscious, onto her bed after her father had beaten her, she had said very softly in case he should hear:

"You will have to go away, Mama. You cannot go on. . .living like. . .this."

"I shall—be all. . .right," her mother had managed to say in a weak, gasping voice.

"No, Mama, you cannot stand it," Ivona had persisted. "This is wrong and wicked! Somebody must speak to Papa and tell him so."

However, her mother continued to say that what was happening was not important and she was not to worry about it.

That Christmas, her mother's father, the *Comte* de Lesmont, had come over from France to stay with them.

Ivona had been delighted to see her grandfather, who was a very distinguished, charming, and intelligent man.

He had brought with him the *Comte* de Gambois, a distinguished relative who was visiting England for the first time since he was a boy.

The *Comte* was rich, charming, and had a family of several children, one of them being a son who he told Ivona was about her age.

"You must come and stay with us in my Château in the Loire," he said. "I know Jean will be only too delighted to show you the countryside."

He smiled as he added:

"Your mother tells me that you love riding, and I think you would find the French horses are just as fast as the English ones."

Her mother had laughed and said how much she would welcome such an invitation.

But Ivona had known even as she spoke that her father was scowling, and it was most unlikely that she would be allowed to go to France.

There had been a large family party that Christmas, for it was traditional for the Marquis's relatives, and there were a great number of them, to gather together at all Festivals.

Afterwards, looking back, Ivona thought she might have been aware that her mother was happier, gayer, and looking more beautiful than she had for a very long time.

Only when all the family had left and her grandfather and the *Comte* de Gambois had gone back to France did Ivona feel as if the fog had closed down again.

Now there were only the incessant Bible readings

and Church-goings to break the silence which seemed to exist between her father and mother.

Then, two months later, her mother received a letter from France in which was enclosed a sketch of the *Comte* de Gambois's son Jean jumping a high hedge.

Ivona thought that not only did the horse look magnificent, but the young man appeared to be riding it superbly.

Because it pleased her, she showed the picture to her father.

"What do you think of this, Papa?" she asked. "I am sure the jump is higher than those we have in England!"

Her father had snatched the sketch from her, stared at it, and said in a voice of thunder:

"Who sent you this?"

Because he was obviously very angry, Ivona replied falteringly:

"It came from. . .the *Comte* de Gambois. . .who came here for Christmas with Grandpapa. It is a. . .drawing of his. . .son."

To her surprise, her father looked at her as if he saw her for the first time, his eyes narrowing, his lips set in a tight line.

"So now you have started!" he said. "Make no mistake, I will beat such tendencies out of you before they grow worse!"

He had flung her to the ground and beaten her cruelly with the same whip that he used on her mother.

For a moment Ivona could hardly believe it was happening.

Then as the whip cracked again and again across her back, cutting through the thin material of the gown she was wearing, she heard somebody screaming and was not aware that it was herself.

Only when later she sobbed convulsively as her mother had sobbed did she say frantically:

"I cannot. . .bear it, Mama! Papa is mad. . .you know he is mad! Take me away. . .oh. . .please. . .take me away!"

Her mother had soothed and comforted her and applied salve to her back which took away some of the pain.

But from that moment Ivona felt that she was walking a tight-rope and that with one unwary step she would fall to destruction:

She thought that her father was beating her mother again when she stayed in bed the next day, unable to move.

She grew thinner and thinner until, frantic with fear that her mother might die, Ivona decided she must write to her grandfather in France.

He was living in Paris now that he had retired from Diplomatic life, and she was certain that if she told him what was happening, he would come back to confront her father.

He would either compel him to refrain from such cruelty or else would take her mother away.

Then, before she could bring herelf to write the letter, feeling it was perhaps disloyal, the news came that her grandfather was dead.

Despite her father's protests that it was unnecessary, her mother insisted that they go to Paris to attend his Funeral.

Reluctantly, being very disagreeable about it, declaring that he personally would never enter a Roman Catholic Church, they crossed the Channel.

It was a long drive to Paris, but to Ivona it was an excitement and a delight to see the French countryside and to hear everybody speak the language which she and her mother used when they were alone.

Actually, on her father's orders, she was not supposed to speak anything but English.

"Ivona is my daughter, and she will speak my language and forget she has any of your blood in her veins!" her father had shouted once, when he had found Ivona and her mother speaking French to each other, not having heard him approach.

After that they were very careful, but because she knew it made her mother happy to speak the language that was her mother tongue, Ivona always spoke it in whispers when they were alone.

She also read French books in the secrecy of her bedroom and said her prayers in French.

After they crossed the Channel, her mother chatted away in French to the servants and the coachman, and when they arrived in Paris she spoke French to her relatives, and Ivona was delighted when they told her that she too spoke like a Frenchwoman.

Except for her hair, they said, nobody would ever have guessed that she was English.

Her mother was dark, but Ivona had taken after her father's side of the family and her hair was fair with red lights in it.

Because the red lights seemed more prominent on the curls which framed her small pointed face, her father continually rebuked her for being untidy and insisted that she try to brush her curls into a more Puritanical neatness.

But he could not alter the contrast or her dark eyelashes over eyes that were flecked with gold and which, when she was excited, shone as if they caught the sunshine.

Her French relatives paid her compliments which made her father scowl, but it was not until they returned to England after the Funeral that Ivona learnt how really angry he was.

Although he had not in fact behaved oddly in France, behaving with her mother's relatives with a dignity and a cold aloofness, once they were home he was more violent than he had ever been before.

First, he beat her mother until she had to remain in bed for a week, too ill to move.

Then, almost as if he had been waiting for an excuse, he took violent exception to a gown which one of the girls of Ivona's age had given her when they were in Paris.

"I bought it just before *Grandpère* died," she had said to Ivona, "but as mourning in France is very, very strict and lasts for over a year, by the time I am able to wear it again it will be out-of-date."

She had pressed it into Ivona's hands, saying:

"Take it with you. You will be able to wear it in six months, and because it is the colour of your eyes, you will look very attractive in it."

It was in fact a pale shade of green like the buds of Spring.

Because it looked so lovely, Ivona decided to try it on, and was walking from her own bedroom towards her mother's to show it to her.

She met her father in the corridor just as he was going out riding.

"Why are you dressed like that?" he asked sharply.

"It is a gown I was given in Paris, Papa," Ivona answered. "I wanted Mama to see me in it, but of course I cannot wear it for another five months."

"So you are intending to flaunt yourself in the hope that you will attract some unfortunate man!" her father said harshly.

Ivona looked at him in astonishment.

"Already you are a Delilah, a Lilith, tempting men into desiring your body!" her father raged.

What he was saying did not seem to make sense.

His eyes were dark, and he was obviously working himself into an uncontrollable rage.

For a moment she was too frightened to move or even to breathe.

Then as she turned to run away, her father seized her by the arm, dragged her into the nearest room, which was an unoccupied bedroom, and beat her until her screams echoed throughout the house.

She was half-conscious when she heard her mother cry:

"Stop, George, stop! You cannot do this to Ivona! You must stop!"

"I will stop when I have beaten the devil out of her!" her father roared. "Already she is planning to tempt some man to destruction!"

He struck Ivona again, and as she felt the agony of it

she tried to scream, but her voice seemed suffocated in her throat.

"You will kill her!" her mother cried.

"Perhaps that would be the best thing to do!" her father retorted. "All women are the tools of Satan, and only pain and the fires of hell will purge them of sin!"

He shouted the last words so that they seemed like the roar of thunder.

Then as Ivona's mother went down on her knees beside her, he left them alone.

It was then that the Marchioness of Morecombe made up her mind.

To save her daughter, she knew she must leave her husband and England.

*   *   *

Her mother had told her how essential it was that they should go secretly and that nobody must learn where they were hiding.

"Your father cannot make me return home, my dearest," she said, "but it is the law that he should have charge of you and that you must obey him."

"I could not. . .live with Papa. . .without you, Mama!" Ivona cried.

"I know that," her mother replied. "That is why we have to creep away and hide from him somewhere in France, and I am sure that once we get there, there will be somebody who will help us."

That somebody, Ivona found, was the *Comte* de Gambois.

He was waiting on the quay when their ship docked at Calais, and from that moment everything changed.

Ivona would have been very stupid and unperceptive if she had not realised from the moment she saw her mother and the *Comte* together that they loved each other.

She thought then that it was something she might have guessed before.

But it had never occurred to her that her mother's

happiness the previous Christmas and her strange radiance at her father's Funeral was due to the *Comte*.

As they journeyed across France, the *Comte* explained that he was taking them to a Château he owned in Alsace.

"It is so far away from where any of my family live," he said, "that I am quite certain nobody will know you are there."

"Why do you own the Château?" her mother enquired.

"My grandmother, who was wildly in love with my grandfather, bought it after he died because she could not bear to live in any place where they had been together. She also disliked most of her relations and wanted a life of her own, which she found in Alsace."

He laughed.

"In fact, she became quite a legend in her lifetime amongst the people there who loved her!"

He looked at the Marchioness as he spoke, and Ivona knew that he was thinking that everybody who met her mother would love her too.

Then he went on:

"None of my other relatives has shown any interest in this Château, and it has been closed for years, so I know you will both be safe there."

"You are so kind," Ivona's mother said softly.

Then as the *Comte* looked at her mother, Ivona realised that she had been forgotten and the two people in the carriage with her were lost in a world of their own.

In the first days of happiness at Alsace, surrounded by the beauty of the valleys, the mountains, and the lush greenery, she still found it difficult to realise that she had escaped.

The opportunity had come when her father had said that he wished to go to London to see his Solicitor.

The way he spoke and the way he looked at her mother told Ivona that he was doubtless making alterations to his Will, which concerned her.

Her mother, on the excuse that she wished to visit

the Dentist, had insisted that she and Ivona accompany him.

At first he had protested, then he had given in reluctantly, and they had arrived at Combe House in Park Street late one evening.

Ivona had been rather surprised at the amount of luggage her mother had brought with them, but she supposed it was in case her father stayed longer than they expected, and she made no comment about it.

But as soon as her father had left the house after breakfast the following morning, saying he would not be back until dinner-time, her mother had told her they were leaving.

"Leaving, Mama?" Ivona exclaimed.

"For France."

"Oh, Mama, do you really mean it?"

"There is nothing else we can do, dearest," her mother answered. "I cannot have your father treating you as he did last week, which I know he will do again and again because you are growing so attractive."

"Why should he dislike me for being attractive?" Ivona asked.

There was a pause, and she thought her mother would not give her a truthful answer.

Then after a moment she replied:

"Because he believes that all women set out to tempt men into desiring them as women."

She did not say any more, but Ivona remembered how her father had told her she was a Delilah and a Lilith, and she understood that that was why he was beating her, and that he had beaten her mother for the same reason.

When she thought of the agony she had suffered and the scars still left on her back, she told herself she hated all men.

"They are cruel and brutal," she said.

Then she decided she would never marry and risk being beaten again for something that she could not help.

But the *Comte* had been different.

While Ivona knew he was married and had a family, somehow it did not seem wrong that he should love her mother and treat herself with an affection which she was sure he gave to his own children.

At the same time, however happy they might be when he visited them in the pretty little Château surrounded by a beauty that was a sheer delight to the eye, Ivona never quite forgot that he was a married man.

'Perhaps he treats his wife in a different way from Mama,' she thought, and shivered as if she felt her father's whip on her back.

But the horror of the nightmare of the past began gradually to fade. Because her mother seemed to grow lovelier day by day and the house was always filled with sunshine, as Ivona grew older she began to forget.

The *Comte*'s visits became more and more frequent and lasted longer, and when he was there it was such fun.

They rode beside the river, climbed a little way up the mountains between the fir trees, and went into nearby towns to buy one another extravagant presents.

Sometimes they visited a concert at which an acclaimed musician was appearing, or sat in a box at the Opera House and applauded a performance which would have been acclaimed in Paris or even over the border in Germany.

Because they were in Alsace, Ivona was very aware that, while they were on French ground and surrounded by French people, they were on the frontier of a very different nation—a nation whose characteristics seemed in many ways to resemble her father's.

The French spoke of Prussian brutality even to their own people, of regimentation, and of incessant official interference with personal freedom.

"I am glad I am French, Mama," Ivona said once when she had been listening to the complaints of one of their servants.

"Half-French, darling," her mother had corrected.

"I have no wish to remember the English part," Ivona replied impulsively.

To her surprise, her mother did not smile. She said slowly:

"Although the English beat us in the war with Napoleon, my father always said the British were a fair, just people, not aggressive like the Germans. In fact, my father often said if he had to be conquered by anybody—which God forbid!—he would rather it was by the English than anybody else!"

Ivona did not reply, she only shivered, thinking of her father and feeling that nobody could be more brutal or more cruel.

Her mother had put out her hand to take hers.

"Listen, darling," she said, "your father was not like that when I first married him, and you have to think of him as a sick man who has a damaged brain."

"I do not wish to think about Papa at all."

As if even the idea perturbed her, she jumped up, taking her hand from her mother's, and left the room.

The Marchioness sighed.

Although she knew it had been the right thing to do to take her daughter out of danger, she could not help wondering what would happen to her in the future.

She was known in Alsace as *Madame* de Lesmont and Ivona was referred to as *Mademoiselle*, but she knew that when her daughter was eighteen, which would be in a few months' time, she should really take her place in the Social World they had left behind when they left England.

But Ivona's mother could not think of anybody in the Combe family who would be strong enough to prevent the Marquis from bringing up his daughter the way he wished to do.

She knew that meant, in his own words, "beating the Devil out of her!"

"But how can she stay here forever?" she asked despairingly.

She knew it was something she must discuss with the *Comte* the next time he came to stay.

He arrived a week later, having spent Easter with his family as was expected of him, and then slipping away eagerly to be with the one person he loved with his whole heart.

Because the French accepted that a man should have a "double life" and there should quite normally be two women who mattered to him, the *Comtesse*, although perhaps it hurt her, made no protests when he left.

Because the *Comte* was deeply in love, the time before he reached the little Château in Alsace seemed endless.

Then the Marchioness, looking lovelier than ever, was holding out her arms to him, and for the first few days they could not think of anything but themselves.

Because Ivona had learnt to be tactful, she left her mother and the *Comte* alone as much as possible, turning up only for meals.

She either went riding with a groom to accompany her or climbed up through the fir trees behind the Château.

She would sit there until it was too cold to remain, looking at the mountains on either side of the valley, which were exceedingly beautiful, covered with snow and silhouetted against the spring sky.

As was usual in the Vosges Mountains, the weather alternated between hot sun, snowstorms, and at times a biting wind which seemed to cut like a knife into the throat.

Ivona had developed a cough and the Doctor had suggested to her mother that it would be wiser next winter for her to be in a warmer climate.

"I do not know if that would be possible," she had said reflectively.

At the same time, she determined to ask the *Comte* if they could all go South, perhaps to Nice, for the worst months of the year, which were January and February.

She had mentioned this to Ivona, who had given a cry of delight.

"I have been longing to see the Mediterranean, Mama,

and Nice is very beautiful. . .or so I have always been told."

"I think perhaps it is too sophisticated for us," her mother had replied.

"At least we are not likely to see Papa there!"

Her mother had flushed, and Ivona had added:

"I am sorry, Mama, I should not have said that. But you know as well as I do that Papa would not approve of any place that had a reputation for being gay and beautiful."

"I do not want to talk about it," her mother had said.

The way she spoke told Ivona that she felt as she did, that the past was past and it must not encroach upon their happiness.

Then, as if Providence, having smiled on them for so long, changed course, disaster came.

It seemed impossible to believe that her mother, so beautiful, so pulsating with life, should now be lying alone in the Churchyard.

Only after the Funeral had taken place did Ivona think that perhaps she should have got in touch with her de Lesmont relations and told them of her mother's death.

Because they had been forced to be so secretive concerning their whereabouts in France, and because her mother had no close relatives, such as a brother or a sister, there seemed to be no point, Ivona thought now, in communicating with them.

Moreover, if they learnt the truth, they would be shocked at her mother having been under the protection of the *Comte* de Gambois.

It was of course for his sake and because he was a relative that her mother had always said that her family as well as his must never be aware of their association.

"They would not only disapprove, but they might make trouble," she had said. "In fact, they might think it their duty to tell my husband where I am."

"We want nobody but ourselves," the *Comte* had said firmly. "Let us be content, my darling, just to be together."

He had forgotten Ivona, who had actually thought he was being very wise.

"People talk, and one is never able to stop them," she had told herself. "Sooner or later some busybody would think it their duty to tell Papa."

She was terrified that this might happen, knowing, as her mother had said, that she would be dragged back to England and incarcerated in a house which in retrospect seemed as dark and gloomy as any dungeon.

Fortunately, the *Comte* had given her mother a great deal of money to pay for everything in the Château and to buy anything she required.

He never came to see them without giving some money to Ivona also, and she therefore felt there was no hurry for her to make up her mind as to what she should do.

She could stay where she was, pay the servants, and buy food and anything else that was required for at least a year, if not longer.

What she had not anticipated was that the death of the *Comte* de Gambois would be reported not only in the French newspapers but also in England.

When the *Comte* had come to England at Christmas to stay with them in the country, he had been received by Queen Victoria and decorated for his services to International Relations.

His accidental death had been described in detail, together with the information that the *Comte* had been accompanied by a *Madame* de Lesmont, who was staying with him at his Château, accompanied by her young daughter, *Mademoiselle* Ivona de Lesmont, who was devastated by the tragedy.

The report inevitably attracted the attention of the Marquis of Morecombe.

For four years he had searched for his wife and daughter, determined to punish them for their deceitfulness in running away from him.

He had employed detectives, but, being English, they had proved very ineffectual on the other side of the Channel.

He had therefore sat alone in his house in Bedford-shire, nursing his grievance and his hatred.

When for the first time there was a clue as to their whereabouts, he was fired with a fury that brought the blood pounding to his head and his heart.

When the servants came to tell him that luncheon was ready, they found him dead on the floor from a heart-attack, with *The Times* lying beside him, opened at the page which reported the *Comte* de Gambois's accident.

Ivona, quite unaware of this, had been riding through the snow and returned to the Château feeling a little happier than she had been for the last few weeks.

At first, being without her mother had made her feel frightened by the silence and the loneliness.

Then somehow she had felt that her mother was still with her, still loving her.

In fact, it was as if she were waiting in the next room, ready to laugh at something that had happened or to anticipate with an irrepressible gladness that the *Comte* might be arriving today, tomorrow, or the next day.

As Ivona drew her horse to a standstill, she said to the groom:

"That was a delightful ride, Henri. It is something we must do again tomorrow."

"*Merci, M'mselle,*" Henri replied.

As she dismounted and turned to walk up the steps into the Château, Ivona noticed the tracks of carriage-wheels in the whiteness of the snow and wondered who had come to call.

There had been so few visitors owing to their living such a secret life that anybody who came to the front door was of interest.

She wished she had been at home and hoped that perhaps they would came another day.

Then as she looked into the Hall, she saw a man's top-hat on the chair.

Even before the servants told her there were visitors, she realised that their carriage must have been taken to the stables so that both the coachman and the horses could be out of the cold.

"Who is it?" she asked in a low voice.

"I do not know, *M'mselle*," the man-servant replied, "but they are English."

"English?"

Ivona felt her heart give a sudden throb of fear, and her first impulse was to run away.

She was sure it was her father waiting for her in the Salon.

Then she knew that if it was her father, she would have to face him sooner or later, and for the moment it was impossible to escape.

Without speaking, she handed the servant her riding-whip and gloves, and, holding her head high, conscious that her heart was beating frantically, she walked slowly across the Hall towards the door of the Salon.

Chapter Two

For a moment Ivona felt a wave of relief sweep over her as she saw that it was not her father waiting at the end of the Salon.

Then she realised that it was his younger brother, her Uncle Arthur, whom she had never liked.

She had always thought that because he was a Parson he had encouraged her father in the religious fervour which had made them all so unhappy.

Now as she walked towards him she thought that her uncle was looking at her with almost the same hostile expression on his face that she had seen on her father's the last months before she and her mother had run away.

He was not, however, alone, his wife being with him.

A dowdy little woman, she had the same expression as her husband's, and it made Ivona feel very nervous as she reached them.

"This is a surprise. . .Uncle Arthur!" she managed to say. "I had no idea you knew that I was. . .here."

"You cannot hide indefinitely from righteousness,"

her uncle replied, "and as the Bible says all too truly: 'Be sure your sins will find you out'!"

There seemed to be no answer to this, and Ivona waited in silence until her uncle went on:

"I understand your mother is dead, and I suppose she is buried locally?"

"Yes, Uncle Arthur."

"We should feel sorry for her," his wife interposed, "but as the good Lord has said: 'Vengeance is mine'!"

With difficulty Ivona managed to ask quietly and in a controlled voice:

"How did you know I was here?"

"Your mother's death, with that of her 'paramour,' was reported in the English newspapers."

It was an answer Ivona had not expected, and she thought for the first time that it had been a mistake for her mother to call herself by her own name.

It would have been better if they had chosen an ordinary one which nobody would have recognised.

As if he knew what she was thinking, her uncle said harshly:

"You should know, and I hope it brings you a feeling of sincere remorse, that your mother's infidelity killed your father!"

"Killed him?" Ivona exclaimed.

"Your father, God rest his soul, is dead!"

It flashed through Ivona's mind that now she was free. Then her uncle went on:

"I am now the Marquis of Morecombe and am your Guardian."

Ivona drew in her breath, but before she could speak, her aunt chimed in:

"I hope you are grateful to your uncle for coming all this way to find you and to look after you, as he considers it his duty to do."

"I am quite all right on my own," Ivona said quickly.

The new Marquis drew himself up.

"That may be your opinion, but I cannot contemplate anything so wrong and indeed wicked as to leave a young girl living alone in a house of sin!"

He looked round the beautiful Salon as if it were crawling with snakes and other reptiles as he went on:

"You have obviously been contaminated, poor child, in such an environment, and in the company of two people who have committed adultery and defamed the sanctity of marriage."

Because she could not bear to hear her mother spoken of in such a way, Ivona replied:

"I do not think you understand, Uncle Arthur, but Papa beat both Mama and me with a riding-whip until we could stand such treatment no longer. The only possible excuse for such brutality was that he was not completely sane."

After she had spoken, there was such an expression of fury on her uncle's face that it made her think he was about to strike her.

Instinctively she took a step backwards before he said:

"That vile lie is what I might have expected from somebody who has no respect for her father and whose mother has defamed the very name of womanhood."

He spoke so violently that his wife put out her hand to touch his arm.

"Do not upset yourself, Arthur dear," she said in a low voice. "The poor child has been indoctrinated with evil and therefore does not understand that she is blaspheming against God."

It seemed as if the Marquis relaxed a little, and he answered:

"You are right, my dear, and the life we have chosen for her in the future is the only way she can do penance and earn forgiveness."

"What life you have chosen for me?" Ivona enquired. "And am I to have no say in it?"

"I am your Guardian under the Law of England," her uncle answered, "and you will therefore do what I say and go where I send you. I can only pray that you will learn to be grateful for the chance of redemption."

"Whatever you have decided," Ivona replied, "I am

now eighteen, and I would like to stay here. . .at least for a. . .little while."

"That is impossible," the Marquis said, "and your aunt and I have no intention of remaining under this roof for one moment longer than is necessary."

"We shall have to stay until tomorrow, Arthur," his wife interrupted in a low voice. "She will not arrive until morning."

"Who will not arrive?" Ivona asked.

"It is not your place to ask questions!" her uncle snapped. "You will learn in due course what has been planned, and I can inform you that your aunt and I have spent long hours worrying over what is best and have asked God's guidance on everything we have decided."

"I am anxious to know what that will be."

Ivona was feeling desperately frightened, as if her uncle was forcing her into a corner from which she had no chance of escape.

Then some pride and a spirit that she had not known she had until now made her want to fight every inch of the way.

Her uncle was silent, but her aunt said:

"I think you should tell her, Arthur, what you have planned."

Her husband looked at her, and Ivona said quickly:

"If you intend to take me back to England, I should like first to get in touch with some of my French relatives. Mama's father is dead, but there are others who, I am sure, would welcome me for her sake."

"Your mother," the Marquis replied, "was most regrettably of French nationality, which is the only possible excuse that can be put forward for her outrageous and disgraceful behaviour."

Ivona wanted to reply, but she felt it was no use, and it would be best to let him tell her what he had planned.

"You will therefore," he went on, "have no contact with your mother's relations, nor do any of your father's wish to see or hear from you again. There is therefore only one way of life open to you in the future."

"And what. . .is that?"

She was frightened and also puzzled by what her uncle was saying.

She knew he was hating her because she could feel his vibrations on the air, which seemed to change and spoil the atmosphere of happiness that had always existed until now in the beautiful Salon.

"I have decided," the Marquis said slowly, "that God must not be mocked, and you will therefore, for your sins and those of your mother, spend the rest of your life—in a Convent!"

There was a pause before the last three words, and as Ivona stared at him in horror and consternation, he went on:

"We have made enquiries, your aunt and I, and we have found there is one near here which will šuit your particular case better than any other. It is the Convent of Haut-Koenigsbourg, which I understand is just the other side of the valley."

Ivona gave an exclamation which seemed to echo round the room.

"But. . .I cannot go there, Uncle Arthur! It is impossible!"

"Nevertheless, that is where you will go!"

"No, you do not understand. . .I have no desire and no vocation to go into a Convent anywhere. . .but the one at Haut-Koenigsbourg is notorious for its. . .severity!"

She drew in her breath before she went on:

"Among its postulants are many young women sent there by the Magistrates because they are considered too young to serve a prison sentence."

Her uncle nodded.

"That is what I have already heard," he said, "and you, my dear niece, will join the postulants to pray for your soul, and that of your mother, so that you shall both, by God's mercy, be saved from eternal damnation."

"You must be mad!" Ivona cried, "as mad as Papa was! I refuse, utterly refuse, to be sent to such a place!"

"You are not to speak to your uncle like that," her

aunt said sharply, "and you have no choice in the matter."

Her voice was shrill, and Ivona thought her uncle was being deliberately vindictive as he said:

"You will either go to the Convent on your own feet or be carried there bound and hand-cuffed, which, as your Guardian, I shall insist upon if the Police have to take you there."

The way he spoke made Ivona feel that he would enjoy seeing her humiliated, and with a superhuman effort at self-control she said:

"Such dramatics will not be necessary. At the same time, I beg of you, Uncle Arthur, to consider, if not my feelings, the fact that as my father's daughter it could cause a scandal that I should be locked away against my will."

As she spoke she knew that such an argument was invalid, for her uncle replied with what she thought was a dangerous glint in his eye:

"You and your mother have already managed for four years to remain anonymous, and when your aunt and I left England nobody knew where we were going."

He smiled before he continued:

"When we return, I doubt if anybody will be interested enough to enquire whether you are alive or dead, and that is exactly what you will be as far as the Combe family is concerned—dead to the world!"

He said the last words as if he were a judge pronouncing sentence.

Just as she had always known in Church in the old days by the way he mouthed over the punishments that would be meted out to sinners in Hell, so Ivona knew that he was thinking with pleasure of how much she would suffer.

As if there was no more to say, her aunt said crisply:

"I think we should now prepare ourselves for dinner, and Ivona can show us where we are to sleep."

She passed down the Salon as she spoke, and added as if she felt compelled to do so:

"I doubt if I shall close my eyes except in prayer! At

the same time, we have had a long journey to get here."

"I will order dinner in an hour's time," Ivona said, "and if you will come with me, I will show you to your room."

She would have turned towards the door, but her uncle's voice stopped her.

"There is one further thing I would add," he said. "If you should try to escape during the night, you will have to do so on foot, and I shall immediately send for the Police to track you down. The horses will be locked up on my instructions and so will your bedroom door."

Ivona thought he must have been reading her thoughts, for she had in fact been determined to run away while they were asleep.

*   *   *

After they had dined on a delicious meal which she could hardly swallow, provided for them by the *Comte*'s Chef, she realised that her uncle was anticipating every move she might make and was prepared for it.

When they returned to the Salon, she had said she would like to retire to bed when he drew a paper from the inner pocket of his coat.

"Before you do so," he said, "I have a document here for you to sign."

"What is it?" Ivona asked.

She suspected it might be her consent to enter the Convent, and she was not certain if it was necessary or not.

Instead, he answered.

"Your Will."

"My. . .Will?"

"Your father left you a considerable sum of money despite the way you treated him."

Ivona was just about to say that she did not want the money and would rather scrub floors than be beholden to her father, when her uncle went on:

"Money is something you will not need in the Convent. I am making them a Grant to ensure that they take you in and keep you there for life, and that is all that is necessary."

"And. . .what are you. . .suggesting I do with the rest of my. . . money?" Ivona enquired.

"You will leave it to me," her uncle said, "and I shall expend it on those who are most in need in my family and amongst the deserving poor."

"I have no wish to leave my money to you or to anybody else in England!" Ivona retorted.

"You will sign this document and not argue," her uncle said sharply. "If you do not do so, I will have you certified as insane, then go to Court and ask that your money revert to me at once, even before your death."

As he spoke, Ivona was certain he was anticipating that she would not live very long.

She remembered that because of her cough during the winter the Doctor had advised that she should go to a warmer climate during the worst months of the year.

She was well aware that the Convent of Haut-Koenigsbourg was very high in the mountains.

Somebody had told her, perhaps it was the *Comte*, that it was twenty-five hundred feet up.

"I shall certainly die if that is where you are sending me," she said involuntarily.

"Then your signature to this will be unnecessary," her uncle replied calmly. "At the same time, I wish to have it, so sign! That is an order!"

He put the document down on the beautiful inlaid *secretaire* which the *Comte* had sent specially from Paris because he knew it would please her mother.

It was there that she had written to him every day when he was away, and Ivona remembered that in the drawer were many bundles of letters he had written to her.

She told herself she must burn them before she left the Château because they were too private to be read by anybody else.

She knew that one person who must never see them was her uncle.

Because it did not seem to matter what she did with

her money since she was not allowed to spend it, she signed the document without reading it.

When she had done so, she knew by the glint in her uncle's eyes that he was delighted at acquiring her money.

She wondered how much she had actually owned but thought it did not matter.

Nothing mattered except that somehow, by some miracle, she must escape from being incarcerated in the Convent at Haut-Koenigsbourg.

When she went upstairs, walking with her uncle and aunt as if already they were her jailors, she was locked in her bedroom and knew despairingly that for the moment there was nothing she could do.

She tried to plan how she could escape tomorrow.

But she could not reach the stables, and even if she did, her uncle's coachman would prevent her from riding away, and therefore she had no idea how she could escape.

She supposed that if she was going to a Convent she would not need any of the beautiful gowns that were hanging in the wardrobe.

The *Comte* had always arranged for her mother to be sent, every few months, the very latest and most elaborate gowns that could be bought in Paris.

At the same time, Ivona also had any gowns she wanted.

He had laughed and said that she and her mother were the most economical women he had ever known.

Only the night before his death, a consignment of Spring dresses had arrived, and now as Ivona opened her wardrobe and saw a kaleidoscope of colour and elegance hanging there, they seemed to mock her.

She heard the key turn in the lock of her room, then her uncle's heavy footsteps walking across the passage to the room he was occupying with her aunt.

Then she felt as if she were in a prison-cell where she would suffocate for want of light and air and, most important of all—love.

"Better to be dead than alive," she said, and then she knew that was the answer to her problem.

She would not go to the Convent and be treated as if she had committed some criminal act, and if she was to be pronounced "dead to the world," it would be far more sensible that she should actually die first.

At least in the next life, if there was one, she would be with her mother and the *Comte*, and even if they were in Hell, as her uncle was convinced they were, at least they would all be together.

"I must die," Ivona told herself, and knew that the real question was "how"?

She looked helplessly round the room as if she thought she would find a gun, a knife capable of piercing her heart, or some other weapon.

But she could see nothing except the beauty of the gowns she would now never wear, her jewellery-case standing on her dressing-table, the lace-edged pillows, and the soft bed in which she had slept every night.

In her vivid imagination she knew only too well what would be her surroundings at the Convent at Haut-Koenigsbourg.

She had in fact visited the Convent of St. Odile in the valley, which was very beautiful and named after the Patron Saint of Alsace.

There the Nuns were sweet, gentle, and very kind. Even though she had no wish to join them, Ivona could understand that life in that Convent might not have been so intolerable as in the one chosen for her so vindictively by her uncle.

Everything she had ever heard about the Convent at Haut-Koenigsbourg came back to her mind now as if to taunt her.

She knew that her uncle was right when he said that the Magistrates sent young girls there to be disciplined when there was not the right sort of accommodation for them in the prisons.

She knew too that the majority of the Nuns were not French but German.

That accounted for the reputation the Convent had

for such strict discipline that to be sent there was almost worse than receiving a prison sentence.

"I cannot bear it, Mama," Ivona said now. "I shall die there, but slowly. Help me to die now. . .quickly, or else to. . .escape as we did. . .before."

But there was no escape, and to jump from her bedroom window would only result in her breaking at least a leg, which certainly was not a sensible thing to do.

*　　*　　*

In the morning, when her uncle had unlocked her door to let her out, she went down to breakfast, after which a Nun arrived.

She was exactly what Ivona might have anticipated a Nun from the Convent of Haut-Koenigsbourg would look like.

A large, gaunt woman in her forties, she spoke with a guttural German accent, and her eyes were hard when she looked at the new postulant who was committed to her charge.

"It was kind of you to come, Sister," the Marquis said genially.

"The Reverend Mother received your letter, My Lord, and the most generous gift to our Convent, for which she thanks you."

The Marquis inclined his head and indicated Ivona.

"This is my niece, who will take the veil after she has been found truly penitent for the many sins she has committed."

He spoke, Ivona thought, like the voice of doom, and the Sister looked her over before she said:

"I have, on the Reverend Mother's instructions, brought with me a habit for the girl to wear. Everything she owns must be left behind."

"Of course, I understand that," the Marquis agreed.

Because she seemed so pleased with the idea, Ivona was quite certain that when she had left, her aunt would have her gowns packed up and take them back to England.

Those that she could not wear herself would doubtless be distributed graciously to the poorer members of the family.

She wanted to cry out at the idea of them gloating over her French clothes and doubtless disparaging them as being too smart.

"I would like to keep a few things that belonged to my mother," she said quickly.

She was thinking of the jewellery her mother had left her, and which she loved because the pieces were so familiar that even to touch them made her feel that her mother was close to her.

"No possessions!" the Nun said sharply. "When you enter the Convent and live for the Glory of God, you renounce everything that is material."

It was hopeless to argue, and Ivona was escorted upstairs by her aunt and the Nun.

As they entered her bedroom the two women seemed almost to be gloating over the fact that she was to leave behind her everything that was beautiful.

For a moment she thought wildly of trying to evade them and running downstairs and out into the snow.

Then she knew that if her uncle failed to prevent her from leaving the house, his servants would catch up with her before she could go very far.

She was wearing only the thin day-gown that she had put on for breakfast and had nothing but slippers on her feet.

Slowly she took off the gown she was wearing, then the beautiful lace-trimmed underclothes, which had also come from Paris, and finally she was forced into a thick cotton chemise that was rough against her skin.

The flannel petticoat she had to put on had been washed until it was stiff and hard, and the dark black robe made her feel it was a shroud that excluded all light from her body.

There was a postulant's veil to wear over her hair, and as the Nun held it out to her, her aunt said:

"Are you not going to cut her hair? I understood that was usual."

The Nun looked at the red-tipped curls that framed Ivona's white and frightened face.

"When she reaches the Convent," she said harshly, "her head will be shaved. There is a special ceremony at which that takes place."

Ivona knew that her aunt was pleased at the answer, but she felt a repugnance that for the moment made her shake as if with an ague.

Then the veil covered her hair, and there was a hood over it to keep out the cold.

When she was ready, wearing a pair of heavy, lace-up black shoes over thick black woollen stockings, her aunt said:

"I would like a word with you, Sister, before we go downstairs."

"Of course, My Lady," the Nun replied.

She walked toward the door to say to Ivona:

"You will stay here until I come to get you."

It was an order, and the sharpness of her tone told Ivona how she would be spoken to in the future.

Her aunt took the Nun across the corridor and into her bedroom.

She left the door slightly ajar, and Ivona crept quietly from her own room to listen to what was being said.

"This girl is wicked, rebellious, and has been perverted by her mother, who was nothing but a harlot!" she heard her aunt say.

"She certainly seems somewhat defiant," the Nun replied.

"My husband understands that you flog those who are unruly."

"If the Reverend Mother considers it necessary, flogging is ordered."

"Will you tell the Reverend Mother that this girl is a persistent liar, and it is my husband's wish that she should be flogged until she confesses her sins and is truly penitent for them."

"I will certainly convey your message, My Lady."

"Thank you, and do not be deceived by her air of innocence, or the lies she will undoubtedly tell you about my poor, lately deceased brother-in-law. It was her mother's behaviour which killed him, otherwise he might be alive today."

"I shall pray for him, My Lady."

"I hope you will do that. At the same time, make quite certain that his daughter does not follow in her mother's footsteps but makes full reparation for the suffering they both have inflicted on an innocent man."

"I will convey to the Reverend Mother everything you have told me, My Lady. The discipline at our Convent is very strict, and we have never yet failed to make the most defiant rebel humble."

"I am sure I can trust you to do exactly as my husband wishes," Ivona heard her aunt say.

Realising that the conversation was at an end, she slipped quickly back into her bedroom.

Once there, she put up her hands to her face and realised she was shaking all over.

She knew it was the thought of being beaten as her father had beaten her.

Like a vision from the past, she could see her mother's face drawn with pain, hear her screams, and feel the sting of the whip on her own skin.

"I must die before it. . .happens again," she whispered. "Help me. . .Mama, help me!"

Then, almost as if her mother answered her, she remembered a conversation which had taken place six or seven years ago, one Sunday after they had come back from Church.

"Everybody in the congregation was either sneezing or coughing," her mother had said lightly as they sat down to luncheon. "I wish Arthur would make the Church a little warmer."

"He believes it does not hurt Christians to suffer for their faith," the Marquis replied.

"I certainly thought that Emily looked extremely ill," her mother went on. "I do not know whether it was because of the cold, but I thought at one moment she might faint."

The Marquis had made a derisive sound as he said:

"There is nothing wrong with Emily except that she takes laudanum every night to make her sleep. I have told Arthur it is a drug he should not allow."

"I agree with you there," his wife had replied. "Too much laudanum can be lethal, and it is very stupid of Emily to take it."

The conversation came back to Ivona's mind now, and she knew, almost as if something had told her so, that was how she could die.

She remembered how after her father's accident he had been given laudanum occasionally.

The Doctor had impressed on her mother that he was only to have a teaspoonful to send him to sleep and relieve the pain when it was intolerable.

Also, the dose was to be repeated only after eight hours.

She waited until the Sister and her aunt came to collect her, then as she walked down the first few stairs behind them she said:

"Forgive me, I have forgotten a handkerchief, and I must have one."

As she spoke she turned and ran up the stairs, aware that it was impossible for them to stop her.

She ran past her own bedroom and into the one in which her aunt had slept the night before, and there on a table by the bedside was what she was looking for.

As she picked up the little black bottle hastily and thrust it inside the habit, she thought there was certainly a lethal dose left in it.

Then she went to her own bedroom and found a handkerchief, and as she took it from a satin sachet scented with a French perfume, she thought that with its lace edging it was very unsuitable for a Convent.

But for the moment she was not concerned with what anybody thought about her or said to her.

She had a way of escape—a way she had been so afraid she would not be able to find.

*   *   *

Ivona and the Nun set out almost immediately, and she learnt that it was going to take many hours to reach the Convent high in the mountains.

The Nun did not expect them to arrive until after four o'clock.

Once they had left the Château and started to climb up the rising road towards the mountainous side of the valley, Ivona was aware that it might take very much longer.

There had been no snow falling when they left. In fact, there was a brief glimpse of the sun coming through the clouds.

Then, as if she had indeed left the sun behind, the clouds seemed to grow darker and heavier and an hour later it began to snow.

She could see very little through the carriage windows, and the Nun sitting stiffly beside her, telling her rosary, was obviously withdrawn into her own thoughts.

They stopped at an Inn a little later to change horses, but Ivona was not allowed to alight, and the Nun gave sharp orders to the coachman to make the change as quickly as possible.

Then they set off again, and now the weather was worse and the horses moved more slowly as the wind blew the snow into their eyes.

It was very cold and Ivona found herself shivering and thinking of the fur coat the *Comte* had given her, which she had loved and which was now hanging in her wardrobe at the Château.

She felt quite certain that her aunt would not leave it there.

"As I am going to die, there is no point in thinking of what I might be wearing," she told herself sensibly.

At the same time, she wished she could die in one of the elegant new gowns with a huge bustle which had just come into fashion.

"For a year, or rather since the end of 1868, the crinoline has been finished," the *Comte* told her mother, "and it is no longer seen in Paris."

Instead, Frederick Worth had introduced the bustle,

and Ivona thought that nothing could be more beautiful than the gowns her mother wore.

They were draped in front, revealing her tiny waist and curved breasts, and billowed out behind like waves following the wake of a ship.

"You look so beautiful, Mama, that you would be the Belle of any Ball!"

"No, that is what you would be, my dearest," her mother answered.

She sighed as she spoke, and they both knew that as things were, there could be no Balls for Ivona, and nobody except the *Comte* to tell her that she was beautiful, and he had eyes only for her mother.

Then, because she did not wish her mother to be introspective or to be worried about her, Ivona put on the gowns which had come from Paris for her mother to see, and which were in the same fashion.

She paraded up and down for her mother's and the *Comte*'s approval, acting for them as if she were on a stage.

They applauded, and as she had run upstairs to put on yet another gown, she thought how happy she was.

She really had no wish to go to Balls, and certainly not to be in the position where anybody might talk of her being married.

"I will never be married," she said aloud, "even if all the Princes and Kings in Europe should ask me to be their wife!"

Because the idea of their doing so was so unlikely and ridiculous, she laughed at her own fantasy.

She had then run downstairs again to show her small audience how pretty she looked in a white gown trimmed with small pink roses with a bustle caught up with bunches of them, and a bow of pink satin ribbon which also encircled her eighteen-inch waist.

Thinking of it as they drove on now, Ivona, feeling the bottle of laudanum resting between her breasts, thought that perhaps in Heaven she would have even more beautiful gowns.

'I cannot believe,' she thought, 'that the angels really wear nothing but shifts which look like nightgowns!'

Then she knew how irreligious her uncle would find such an idea!

Outrageously, she wanted to tell him that her halo, if she had one, would be decorated with diamonds, or if instead she had devil's horns, they would be embellished with rubies and emeralds!

Because she had been so much alone, Ivona lived very much in a fantasy-world, and the tales of witches, goblins, sprites, and elves which were so much part of Alsace had always enthralled her.

Now she wished she knew of a spell so that she could become invisible and disappear, leaving the Nun astonished!

Or, she thought, better still, discover a magic-carpet which would transport her to where she could be with her mother.

Because it seemed a funny idea, she wanted to laugh, but she was quite certain that if the Nun knew what she was thinking, she would consider it extremely blasphemous.

Suddenly and quite unexpectedly the horses came to a standstill.

The Nun, who had actually been dozing a little, opened her eyes and asked crossly:

"What is happening? Why have we stopped?"

There was the sound of a number of people all talking at once, and as the Nun struggled to let down the window of the coach, the door opened.

"*Pardon*, Sister," said one of the men who had been driving, "but we can go no farther."

"What do you mean—no farther?" the Nun enquired.

"The road is blocked with snow."

"I do not believe it."

"You can see for yourself, Sister. You could not get an elephant along this road, let alone a horse!"

The Nun stood up and put her head out the door.

Ivona wondered where they were and whether there

was a chance of her escaping away into the darkness before anybody could prevent her.

Then another man came to the side of the carriage to say:

"There's an Hotel, *Madame*, about half a kilometre to the left. You will have to stay there until we clear the road."

"An Hotel!" the Nun exclaimed in a voice of horror.

"There's nowhere else, *Madame*, and they say they will have cleared the road by tomorrow morning, unless there's another snow-storm."

The Nun gave in with a bad grace.

"Very well, tell the coachman to take us there."

It was obviously difficult to turn the horses, but somehow they managed it, and after a slow, bumpy ride there were the bright lights of a small Hotel and the horses drew up outside it.

For a moment, an irresistible hope flared up within Ivona that this was the place from which she might escape.

Then, as if such an idea were crushed by a heavy hand, she knew that dressed as she was, and with no money, she had not the slightest chance of succeeding.

"There is no alternative," she told herself. "I must die!"

Chapter Three

There were a number of people who were stranded, like themselves, in the Hall of the Hotel.

Looking at them, Ivona realised they were mostly businessmen, doubtless on their way to Strasbourg, and there were very few women.

As they entered, everybody's eyes went towards the Nun and herself, then as if they felt they should not be inquisitive about anybody wearing the dedicated robes of chastity, they looked away again.

The man who had spoken to them in the road took the Nun up to the desk and explained that they would require bedrooms for the night.

"One bedroom!" the Nun snapped.

"That makes it easier, Sister," replied the man behind the desk.

"And as cheap as possible," the Nun added firmly. "I come from the Convent of Haut-Koenigsbourg, and we do not spend money carelessly."

"That is very commendable, Sister."

He produced a key, which he handed to a man standing beside him, saying as he did so:

"Show the ladies to Room Thirteen!"

Ivona thought the number was appropriate.

At the same time, she was worrying as to how she could take her life if she was sleeping in the same room as the Nun.

Then she thought that the older woman was sure to sleep heavily, and that would give her a chance to do what she had planned.

They walked up the stairs to where all the Hotel bedrooms opened off one long landing.

The man showing them the way walked towards the very end of it, and Ivona had the idea that it would be one of the cheapest and most uncomfortable bedrooms in the Hotel.

They had almost reached the door when a valet came along the corridor, carrying in his hand a pair of highly polished gentleman's boots.

Ivona thought they looked a very small size and wondered to whom they belonged.

Then as they reached their own room, another valet appeared from the room opposite them to say:

"Hurry up, Gustave, the young master is waiting."

The valet with the boots disappeared into the room, and the Nun and Ivona were shown into Number 13.

It was sparsely furnished but spotlessly clean, and contained two beds side-by-side, with a window that looked out onto the back of the Hotel.

"I hope you will be comfortable, Sister," said the man who had shown them there, "and dinner will be ready almost immediately."

He did not wait for a reply, but shut the door, and only when he was out of hearing did the Nun say, as if she spoke to herself:

"I think it would be good for us both to fast, and to pray that the snow will soon be cleared."

Instinctively Ivona gave a little cry.

"I am very hungry," she said, "as I was unable to eat any breakfast this morning."

As she spoke, she remembered that her uncle and aunt had not offered the Nun any refreshment when she came to the Château.

It was unlike the way her mother would have behaved but was typical, she thought, of her aunt's and uncle's mean nature.

She was sure, therefore, that the Nun too was hungry, although she did not say any more.

The Nun took off the heavy cloak she had worn for travelling with its hood which pulled forward over her wimple and veil.

Then she washed in cold water which she poured from the ewer into a bowl on the washing-stand in the corner, and after she had finished, Ivona did the same.

She found it difficult to concentrate on anything except how she could kill herself in these surroundings.

She was sure that if the Nun saw her drinking the laudanum, the bottle of which still lay heavily between her breasts, she would prevent it.

What was more, it was absolutely essential that the dose she took should be effective.

She had heard stories of how women had tried to commit suicide but had been saved from dying by being taken to Hospital.

'I must be certain that the laudanum kills me,' she thought.

She was still thinking about it when a gong boomed through the Hotel, announcing to everybody that dinner was ready.

"We will go down at once," the Nun said sharply, to Ivona's surprise, "and eat quickly, as we must rise very early tomorrow. The Reverend Mother will be extremely perturbed at our delay."

Ivona thought there would be still further delay when she was found dead in the morning.

She followed the Nun downstairs and into the Dining-Room, which had windows overlooking what she guessed was a beautiful view at the front of the Hotel.

But now it was dark and there was nothing to see

except some very distant lights and the stars coming out overhead.

Ivona was aware that the snow had stopped and the wind had dropped. She knew that later, when the clouds had cleared, there would be a full moon.

Then with a little sigh of regret she thought that she would not see it.

At the same time, she was afraid it would enable the men who were clearing the road to do so more quickly than if the weather had still been bad.

She and the Nun were allocated a table in a corner of the room and the menu was set in front of them.

"Would it be cheaper if we had one dish instead of the whole menu?" the Nun asked the waiter.

"Tonight, Sister, as there are so many extra guests," he replied, "there will be nothing *a la carte* except for *pâté* for those who can afford it."

Ivona knew that because they were near Strasbourg the *pâté de foie gras* was the best in all France, but because it was so good it was also expensive.

"We will have the menu," the Nun said in an uncompromising voice, and waved away the suggestion that they should drink wine with their meal.

Although the Hotel was small, the food was delicious, as was usual in France. As she ate, Ivona was glad that her last meal was palatable.

The Nun certainly found it so, and because she was German she helped herself greedily, filling her plate with food.

Ivona guessed that the food at the Convent would be sparse, and she had the idea, although she could not be certain, that she had once heard that they starved those who were refractory.

It was difficult to be revolutionary or aggressive when one's body was weak from hunger.

"Whatever happens, I shall not be there to be treated in such a manner," she told herself.

Because she was eating so much less than the Nun was, she had time between courses to look round at their fellow-guests.

Those who had been stranded unexpectedly looked more affluent than the usual travellers to stay in such a place, and Ivona noticed that they ordered expensive bottles of wine.

As they were finishing their meal, into the Dining-Room came three men.

They were distinctive not only because in their features and bearing they looked aristocratic, but also because, unlike anybody else in the room, they had changed for dinner.

The first was a very distinguished elderly man with grey hair, and the next, who was a little younger, also had an air of nobility about him. The third was a young man of about her own age, Ivona thought, and as soon as she saw him she knew it was his boots that had been cleaned by the valet.

He was dressed in the very height of Parisian fashion in clothes similar to those the *Comte* had always worn, and she thought he was rather good-looking.

But while he interested her, she quickly saw how important his party was, because as soon as they were seated the Chef came from the kitchen to discuss what they would wish to eat.

The table at which they sat was quite near to Ivona's, so she could hear what they were saying, and there was obviously no question of their having the menu.

They were starting with *pâté de foie gras* and after that they were having blue trout from the glacier streams flowing down from the mountains.

The roe-deer which the Chef described in detail would be cooked for them in a very special way with red wine, and there were a number of other dishes which Ivona knew she had often enjoyed at the Château.

After they had given their order there was a prolonged discussion as to which wine would go best with each course.

Because as she listened she was staring at the three men, Ivona discovered that the young man was looking at her curiously.

Their eyes met and she felt, to her annoyance, that

he was sorry for her because she was dedicated to a life of chastity.

She looked away and it flashed through her mind that perhaps she might ask the three men for help.

Then she knew it would be quite hopeless.

Even if they were willing to help her, her uncle was still in the vicinity, and all the decisions he had made regarding her were within the law.

When it occurred to her that possibly she might appeal to somebody who would understand her predicament, hope had flickered in her heart, but now she felt the darkness descend upon her again.

The Nun pushed back her chair.

"Come," she said. "It is time we went upstairs."

It was the first time she had spoken to Ivona since they had sat down to dinner, which she had started with a long Grace, crossing herself as she finished.

Now she stalked towards the door, and there was nothing Ivona could do but follow her.

Just before she reached it she had an idea, and she deliberately hung back to say in a low voice to the watier who was bowing them out:

"Will you please send some coffee to Room Thirteen?"

"*Certainement, M'mselle,*" he replied.

When she smiled at him she knew that, despite the veil over her hair and the cumbersome black robe, there was a glint of admiration in his eyes.

Therefore, she was certain as she followed the Nun upstairs that he would obey her request.

She had quickly decided that this was the way she would be able to drink the laudanum without the Nun being aware of it.

The Nun had locked the door when they went down to dinner and now she fumbled in the depths of her black robe to find the key.

As she did so, the valet whom Ivona had seen before came out of a bedroom opposite.

He pushed open the door next to it and shouted:

"Come on, Gustave! Our supper's ready. If you don't hurry, half the dishes will be off the menu!"

"I'm coming!" Gustave replied. "I'll finish later."

He came out into the passage as he spoke, and after pulling the door to behind him he hurried after the other valet down the stairs.

By this time the Nun had found the key, and as Ivona followed her into the bedroom she locked the door and walked across to the bed nearest the window.

"I will sleep here," she said, and pulled the bed farther away from the one next to it.

She took off her veil and wimple, and Ivona saw that her hair was almost white and painfully thin and her forehead was very high.

But Ivona after one look was waiting, hoping the coffee would soon arrive.

Even as she thought of it there was a knock on the door.

The Nun started.

"What is that?"

"Shall I see for you, Sister?" Ivona enquired.

Because the Nun had already begun to undo her habit, there was nothing she could do but agree.

She held out the key, which she had put down on her bed.

Ivona took it from her, unlocked the door, and opened it.

The waiter to whom she had spoken was standing outside with a tray on which there were two cups and a pot of coffee.

"Thank you very much," Ivona said.

She realised she had nothing with which to tip the man, but he obviously did not expect it, and said with the same look of admiration in his eyes:

"It's a pleasure, *M'mselle!*"

She took the tray from him, holding it with one hand as she shut the door.

"Coffee?" the Nun exclaimed. "I did not order it, and doubtless it is extra."

"I am sure, Sister, it is with the compliments of the Manager," Ivona replied, "and it was very gracious of him. You can hardly refuse to accept it."

"I suppose, as it is here, we may as well drink it," the Nun said grudgingly.

Ivona put the coffee down on a table which was near the door, and as she did so the Nun added:

"Lock the door and bring me the key."

She spoke in a disagreeable tone, as if she had already caught Ivona trying to escape from her.

As she did as she was told, Ivona thought once again that escape was an impossibility, seeing the way she was dressed.

She handed the key to the Nun, who looked grotesque in her coarse chemise of the same material as that which Ivona had been forced to wear and a thick flannel petticoat.

"I will pour out the coffee for you," Ivona offered.

She placed it so that to do so she had her back to the Nun, who could not see what she was doing, and slipping her hand inside her bodice she brought out the small black bottle.

She wondered if it would act very quickly so that she could die wearing her habit and at least not looking as unpleasant as the Nun did.

Then as she picked up the coffee-pot to begin pouring out the first cup, she had a sudden idea.

It was so fantastic that for a moment she thought it was foolish even to contemplate such a thing. Then, almost as if it were a jig-saw puzzle, the idea multiplied itself and each piece fell into place.

Slowly she filled the cup, knowing as she did so that her heart was pounding like the strokes of a gigantic clock, and she was so excited that it was difficult to breathe.

She almost filled the cup, then poured half the contents of the bottle of laudanum into it and added several spoonsful of sugar, stirring it round.

Then, hiding the bottle behind the coffee-pot, she carried the cup across the bedroom to the Nun.

She had taken off her heavy shoes, but it appeared that she did not intend to undress any further, and was putting her rosary on the bed in front of her preparatory to saying her prayers.

"You must drink this while it is hot, Sister," Ivona said. "I think it is going to be very cold tonight, and there is no way of heating this bedroom."

As she spoke she realised that the room was already extremely cold, which explained why it was cheap.

As if the Nun was aware of it too, she glanced towards the window, shuddered, then took the cup of coffee and started to drink, as Ivona watched her tensely.

She had no idea if laudanum had any taste, but she was sure that such a large dose would work quickly, and unless the Nun was very different from her father, she would undoubtedly sleep for nearly twenty-four hours before she awoke.

But she also was sure that she had not given her a lethal dose, which was what she had intended for herself.

The cup was now empty, and because the Nun had gulped it down, it was doubtful that she had tasted anything.

She handed the cup back to Ivona and said:

"As it is so cold, I shall say my prayers in bed, but as you are younger you will kneel in the prescribed position and ask God's forgiveness."

"Yes, Sister," Ivona said humbly.

She carried the empty cup back to the table, then poured a little coffee into the other cup.

It was very strong, which usually she did not like.

But she drank it, hoping it would sweep away her tiredness and make her able to carry through her plan, which required both strength and concentration.

She sipped the coffee slowly, turning round as she did so to watch the Nun.

She had got into bed and pulled the blankets up to her chin. Already her eyes were closed, but Ivona was not sure whether that was because she was praying or whether the laudanum was already doing its work.

Then as she finished the coffee the Nun began to snore, and as she did so Ivona remembered it was the same sound that her father had made when he had been given laudanum after his accident. It was not an ordinary snore but a kind of rasping one.

Then after a little while the sound sank lower into a kind of rhythm which told Ivona that the Nun was deeply asleep and it would be impossible to awaken her.

She wasted no time as she picked up the key which the Nun had placed on a small table beside her bed while she drank her coffee, together with the small oil-lamp that was burning there also, unlocked the door, and walked out into the passage.

There was nobody about, but the noise of voices came from the Dining-Room downstairs.

She slipped like a dark shadow into the bedroom where she had seen the valet carry the young man's boots.

She found, as she expected, that the clothes he had discarded when he changed for dinner were laid out on a chair.

His overcoat, which was a very fashionable one with a tiered cape, was hanging up in the wardrobe, the door of which was open.

Ivona shut the door and quickly took off the clothes which she had been forced to put on when she left the Château.

The young man's trousers were a little tight for her, but she struggled into them, put on his fine linen shirt with his high collar, and wound the long tie round her neck to tie it in a bow at the front.

His cut-away coat with its long tails had been placed on the back of a hard chair, but just as she was about to put it on Ivona had another idea.

The brushes with which he was travelling were laid out on the dressing-table, as was a folded leather case which was exactly like the one the *Comte* had brought with him in his dressing-case every time he came to the Château.

She opened it now and saw that it contained two folded razors, a nail-file, and beside them, what she was searching for, a pair of scissors.

There was a looking-glass hanging on the wall, and after pulling out the hairpins which had kept her hair in place under the veil, she started to cut off her long tresses as quickly as she could.

The scissors were sharp, and she threw the pieces of fair hair tinged with gold on top of the black habit which lay on the floor.

She cut her hair to the right length for a fashionable young man, and because it was curly it did not look uneven, and she knew that once she was outside the ends would tighten in the air and curl all over her head.

However, as she finished she did not put back the scissors but slipped them into her pocket.

Picking up the robe, the veil, and the heavy shoes she had worn, she bundled everything on top of the wardrobe, then pressed them down until they were out of sight.

Quickly she put on the young man's top boots which the valet had cleaned until they shone almost like black mirrors, the tail-coat, and over it the overcoat which was hanging in the wardrobe.

Glancing round the room, she saw a top-hat and a pair of gloves lying on a chest, and picked them up before she blew out the lamp.

As she opened the door, she saw to her relief that there was nobody in the corridor, but the difficulty now was to get out of the Hotel without being seen.

It was impossible to go through the Hall, where somebody was certain to be on duty, or perhaps some of the guests, having finished their meal, would be sitting in front of the big log fire.

She knew where the Dining-Room was situated, which gave her some idea of where the kitchen was, and she deliberately walked along to the other end of the corridor.

As she had hoped, there was a smaller, secondary staircase going down to the ground floor, and having walked down it she found herself in another straight corridor at the end of which was the Hall.

On the other side of it a door stood ajar, and one glimpse inside the room told her it was a small Writing-

Room for Resident guests and at the moment it was empty.

She went in, closed the door behind her, and pulled back the curtains over the window, which she then opened.

When she looked out she saw that it was the back of the Hotel, where the rising ground was nearer to the window than it was in the front.

It was also white with snow.

Ivona wasted no time as she climbed first onto a chair, then onto the window-sill, and let herself out the window.

It was only a short drop to the ground, and although the snow was over the ankles of her boots, it was not difficult to walk in them.

She moved quickly away from the lights of the Hotel, then paused to take her bearings.

She had already made up her mind that the only sensible thing she could do would be to try to make her way back to the Château.

She was quite certain that once she was there, the servants who had looked after her mother and herself ever since they had come to France would hide her.

She would also be able to find some of her own money, if her uncle and aunt had not removed it, and of course her own clothes.

There were a great many risks and problems attached to the idea, but she could think of no alternative.

Resolutely she skirted round the back of the Hotel, crossed the road, and set off down a path lined with trees.

She had not been wrong in thinking there would be a moon, and now it was quite bright, although it would be considerably stronger later on.

Because the ground in front of her was sloping downwards, the snow was not deep enough to go over the tops of her boots. But she had to move carefully, in case she should trip over something buried under the snow and twist her ankle or even break a leg.

Soon she was clear of the trees and now she could see a huge patch of untouched snow in front of her.

She realised that the Hotel was high up, higher than she had thought it to be, although she knew that the horses had been climbing for a long time before they reached the road that was blocked.

She felt she must be past the place where they had come to a halt, and she knew that the best thing she could do was to find her way to the road which would lead her back through the valley to the Château.

As they had been travelling all day, she was aware that it must be many miles away.

But it was important that she should walk as far as she possibly could during the night so that when they began to search for her they would not expect her to have got so far away.

She walked on and on, the trees on one side of her, the snow on the other.

She reasoned out that it would be wise to keep near to the trees so that her footsteps would not show in the snow.

Besides, she was quite certain it would be far deeper on the other side where there was nothing to break its fall.

The trees began to grow thicker, and as she thought they were part of a wood, she wished that when she had been travelling along the road she had been able to see what was on either side.

She was sure she was going in the right direction, and yet, because the walking was difficult and with every step she had to pull her feet out of the deep snow, she began to grow very tired.

She was also extremely cold, and her small nose felt as if it did not belong to her.

But she forced herself on, knowing that as she had left the bottle of laudanum behind her, that way of escape was now lost to her.

If she was caught, the only thing left would be to die in the Convent as her uncle hoped she would do.

Half-an-hour later she was beginning to think that it

would be impossible to go any farther and she would
have to rest.

At the same time, she was intelligent enough to know
that if she did sit down, she would soon be frozen stiff
and unable to move.

It was then, for the first time since leaving the Hotel,
that she saw a light.

It was not very strong, but it was definitely a light,
and it came from between the trees on her left.

Almost as if she was drawn to it mesmerically, Ivona
moved towards it, then realised it was not a house, as
she had at first thought, but a hut.

She knew immediately that it was a wood-cutter's hut
such as those that the *Comte* had in his woods round
the Château.

She had been into some of them and felt they were
almost like little doll's-houses, with a fire where the
wood-cutters could warm themselves and cook a meal.

Sometimes the men cut trees there into planks to
make chairs and tables.

As she drew nearer, she saw that the log hut was
strongly made and was aware there was smoke coming
out from the chimney.

The thought of a fire made her realise how terribly
cold she was.

She was sure that if there was a wood-cutter there,
she could persuade him to let her sit by his fire before
she must once again be on her way.

She thought that if there was more than one man,
they might be talking or perhaps asleep.

With difficulty, because her hand was numb, she
lifted the latch on the door, which was made from
trunks of trees, and pulled it open.

Because the light from the fire was very bright, for
the moment it was difficult to see.

Then she was aware that there was a man on the
other side of the hut, sitting on the ground, his legs
stretched out in front of him.

"May I please. . .come in?" she asked.

As she spoke she realised that the man to whom she was speaking was certainly not a wood-cutter.

He was looking at her in surprise, and she saw that he was a handsome man and certainly was a gentleman.

He was wearing a heavy overcoat with a fur collar, but his head was bare, and as she waited for his answer, Ivona walked farther into the hut.

"I am delighted to see you!" the gentleman said. "But I am somewhat surprised to have visitors at this time of night in such an outlandish place!"

Ivona shut the door and, moving towards the fire, said:

"I am cold. . .so very cold that I could not go on. . .walking any. . .farther!"

"Then I am very pleased to share my fire with you."

Ivona did not answer because she had realised that when she spoke her teeth were chattering.

Now she knelt down beside the fire and held out her hands to it, aware that even though she was wearing gloves, she could not feel her fingers.

She could think of nothing at the moment except that the warmth was the most delightful sensation she had ever known, and gradually she could feel first her hands, then her nose.

Only when she had knelt for some minutes did she pull off her gloves and put them down beside her, then hold out her hands towards the warmth of the fire again.

At last, as if she became aware that the man sitting on the floor was watching her, she turned her head to look at him.

He was definitely even better-looking than she had thought at first.

At the same time, she told herself, he was not a very young man, but she was sure he was rich.

It was not only that he wore an expensive overcoat, but there was some assurance about him which made her certain that he was not only important but wealthy.

Then, because it seemed strange that he should be sitting in a wood-cutter's hut, she said:

"I expected to find. . .somebody very. . .different in. . .here."

"You have been here before?"

"No, of course not. It was just that I could see it was a hut used by the wood-cutters."

"Naturally!" the gentleman said. "And now that you are feeling less like an icicle, I suggest we introduce ourselves, and I admit to being curious as to how you managed to find this place."

Ivona smiled faintly.

She was trying frantically to remember the story she had thought up as she was walking along, to explain why, dressed as she was, she was without a carriage and without money.

Before she could speak, the gentleman said:

"I am the *Duc* de Sancerre!"

Ivona started. As he spoke, she knew exactly who he was, and was aware that the name she was about to call herself would be most inappropriate.

She had in fact thought that as the *Comte* had a son of about her own age, she would tell anybody who asked her that she was Jean de Gambois.

She now realised that as she had heard the *Comte* speak of the *Duc* de Sancerre, he might have seen Jean, and would know that she did not resemble him.

Because her mother and she were still in hiding, they had never met any of the distinguished people in Alsace, although the *Comte* had often spoken of them.

Ivona had been fascinated when he told her of the beautiful Palace which the *Ducs* de Lorraine had built at Stanislas.

She had always longed to see what was a small-scale replica of the Palace of Versailles, in which, in the Eighteenth Century, the *Duc* had emulated, on a more modest scale, the magnificence of the French Court.

The other most important man in the neighbourhood was the *Dec* de Sancerre.

"His Château is fantastic!" Ivona remembered the *Comte* telling her mother. "I wish, my darling, that I could show it to you."

"I am more than happy with your Château," her mother had answered softly, and for the moment the *Duc* de Sancerre was forgotten.

But his name had often cropped up in their conversation.

There was an occasion when his horses beat the *Comte*'s at Chantilly, and Ivona remembered that he had given a ball to which the *Comte* had to escort his wife and so was obliged to cut short his visit to them and return to Paris.

Quickly now she thought of the first name that came into her head and said:

"My name is Bethune."

"Then why, *Monsieur* Bethune," the *Duc* asked, "if it is not an indiscreet question, are you walking about alone at this time of night?"

With a little sigh, Ivona took off her top-hat and made herself more comfortable as, thinking quickly, she replied:

"Terrible. . .things have. . .happened to me!"

"I am interested to hear what they are."

"I was travelling with my Tutor, a horrible man chosen for me by my uncle, who I am quite convinced was instructed to kill me!"

"To kill you?" the *Duc* exclaimed.

Ivona nodded.

"My uncle did not say so, but it is because I inherited my father's title. He was the *Comte* de Bethune, and I also inherited all his money. If I should die unmarried and without a son, everything would go to my uncle, and so he was determined to dispose of me."

"I can hardly believe that what you are telling me is true!" the *Duc* exclaimed.

"Unfortunately, it is true," Ivona insisted. "They were deliberately sending me to stay in the mountains, although the Doctors had ordered me to the South of France where the climate is warmer!"

She paused, then as the *Duc* did not speak, she went on:

"If I did not die of the cold, then I think my Tutor had instructions to make certain I did not return home."

"So you escaped from him!" the *Duc* said.

"We were held up by robbers on an isolated part of the road when it was snowing. My Tutor began to fight with them, and while he was doing so, I ran away and hid amongst the trees."

"You have been most unfortunate," the *Duc* said, "for I have not heard of anybody being robbed in such a way recently, although it has been known to happen in the past."

"It was very frightening!" Ivona agreed. "But at least I am alive."

"And what do you intend to do with yourself?" the *Duc* asked.

Ivona hesitated. Then, because she felt he might be able to help her, she said:

"If it is possible, I want to get to Paris."

As she spoke, she thought that if she could reach Paris, she would find her mother's relatives.

She was sure that if they knew her circumstances they would not refuse to help her, however much they might disapprove of her mother's association with the *Comte*.

"To Paris!" the *Duc* remarked. "But you say you have no money?"

"Not a cent!" Ivona replied. "My Tutor saw to that!"

"It is certainly a very sad story."

The *Duc* spoke in a dry, somewhat cynical voice, which made Ivona think that he did not really believe what she was saying.

At the same time, as he was her one hope, she turned to him and said pleadingly:

"Please. . .please. . .help me. . .and promise me you will not. . .tell my uncle where I am."

"If you ask me to keep your secret, I must of course agree," the *Duc* replied.

Her eyes lit up in the firelight.

"Do you mean that? Then I am very, very grateful, and it is what I might have expected."

The *Duc* raised his eye-brows.

"You speak as if you have heard of me."

"I have heard of your horses and the many races they have won, and of course of your Château, which I have been told is very magnificent."

"I hope you will think so when we reach there," the *Duc* replied.

"You mean. . . ?" Ivona began, then exclaimed: "But how selfish of me! I have not asked you why you are here."

"It is quite simple," the *Duc* said. "I was skiing, and I fell and sprained my ankle."

"Skiing? Do you mean gliding over the snow on two planks of wood?"

"A good way to describe it," the *Duc* laughed, "but I am surprised that you have heard of it."

Ivona was just about to say that the *Comte* had talked of trying it after reading reports of skiing in Norway.

But her mother had discouraged him from doing so because she thought it was dangerous.

"Is it difficult to do?" she asked impulsively.

"It is difficult," the *Duc* replied, "because the 'planks of wood,' as you call them, are difficult to keep attached to one's feet, which is why I have hurt myself, although I expect really it was through my inefficiency."

"I believe people have been trying to walk on snow since the very early days."

The *Duc* smiled.

"I can see you are well read. The Germans experimented with it early in the Sixteenth Century, but it certainly is something new to the French."

"I would like to see you do it."

"Unfortunately, it is impossible at the moment," the *Duc* answered, "since it will take time for my ankle to heal, and time is something we have not got."

The way he spoke made Ivona look at him in surprise.

Then, when she was about to question the rather strange note in his voice, she said:

"If you really have a sprained ankle, you should take

off your boot, otherwise your leg will swell and will have to be cut off."

"I have anticipated that already," the *Duc* said, "but I am hoping that help will soon be at hand."

Then, before Ivona could ask what he meant, the door opened and a man came in.

He was wearing a thick overcoat collared with fur, and he had a fur hat which made him look strange and, Ivona thought, rather like the pictures she had seen of Russians.

"You are back!" the *Duc* exclaimed. "Thank God for that!"

"The carriage is on the road about a hundred yards from here," the newcomer said, "and I have two men outside, ready to carry you there."

As he spoke, he looked at Ivona curiously, and the *Duc* said:

"Let me introduce you to my visitor, who has also found sanctuary here—the *Comte* de Bethune—the *Vicomte* de Valmont!"

The *Vicomte* was looking at Ivona with astonishment before he said:

"Life is certainly full of surprises! Incidentally, Jules, I found our friend, and he confirms everything he said before, and is quite certain we have no more than two months' respite, perhaps less!"

He spoke in a voice which made Ivona quite certain that what he was saying was secret and of great importance to the *Duc*, who nodded before he replied:

"That is exactly what I anticipated. You recompensed him, of course?"

"I was generous, exactly as you told me to be," the *Vicomte* answered, "and he was in fact very satisfied."

"Good!"

"He promised that if there were any further developments," the *Vicomte* went on, "he would somehow get in touch with you at the Château, unless you had already left for Paris."

"Thank you," the *Duc* said. "And now, for God's

sake, get me home! My leg is beginning to be damned painful."

Ivona was surprised at the way he swore.

Then she remembered that the *Duc* thought she was a young man, and not a woman, otherwise he certainly would not have used such language in front of her.

"It is something I must not forget," she told herself.

The *Vicomte* had opened the door of the hut and she heard him give an order to the men who must have been waiting outside.

Two men in the *Duc*'s livery came into the hut, making it seem very overcrowded.

Because in order to reach the *Duc* they had to pass her, she rose to her feet, picked up her hat and gloves, and stood on one side.

"The *Comte* is coming with us," the *Duc* said to the *Vicomte*. "He is in even more desperate trouble than I am, and I have promised to help him."

The *Vicomte* smiled.

"You look very young," he said to Ivona, "to be in the sort of trouble I anticipate."

For a moment she did not understand.

Then she remembered that the *Duc* had a reputation not only as a sportsman but as a *roué*.

In fact, she could recall her mother saying once:

"I see the *Duc* de Sancerre's horses have beaten yours again."

"I know," the *Comte* had said ruefully, "but Sancerre always has the best of everything—horses, houses, and beautiful women! And that, my darling, is why under no circumstances will I ever allow you to meet him!"

Her mother had laughed.

"Can you really be so stupid as to be jealous?" she asked. "If there are any other men in the world besides you, I am not aware of them."

"That is what I want to hear you say," the *Comte* replied. "At the same time, Sancerre seems to be invincible, and if I had to fight a duel with him over you, I have the unfortunate feeling that I would be the loser."

"There will be no duel!" her mother replied. "And you will never lose me as long as you want me."

They had not been aware that Ivona was in the room because she was curled up in a window-seat reading a book.

Now she remembered listening, and after the *Comte* had kissed her mother she had said:

"How could any man mean to me what you mean? And I am quite certain that you are far more handsome, far more attractive, than any *Duc* could be."

"Say that again," the *Comte* pleaded in a deep voice. "At the same time, my precious, I am sorry that I cannot show you his Château near here, and his treasure-house, for it is nothing else, in the Champs Élysées."

"Possessions are not important," her mother said.

"That is what Sancerre says, but it is not true. He enjoys being the most envied man in France, and just as he collects pictures and objets d'art and the fastest horses ever bred, he also collects beautiful women. So I repeat, I would never allow him to set eyes on you."

"And what do beautiful women feel about him?"

"They fall at his feet in ecstasy if he so much as looks at them, and they cry despairingly when he breaks their hearts and leaves them for somebody even more beautiful than they are."

"He sounds abominable!"

"Of course he is," the *Comte* agreed, "so think only of me, and know that I shall love you from now until eterntiy."

Ivona remembered afterwards being very curious about the *Duc*'s Château, but not particularly so about him.

Now as he was lifted from the ground by his two servants and carried out of the hut and along the side of the trees where the snow was not too deep, she followed behind him.

She had become warm as she sat by the fire, but she was instantly conscious of the frosty air biting at her as if it would turn her once again into an icicle.

Then as she saw the carriage waiting by the roadside, she knew she had been saved in a positively miraculous fashion, and there was a warm feeling in her heart which had not been there before.

She was quite certain now that it was her mother who had saved her from killing herself by her own hand, as she had intended to do, saved her from being taken to the Convent at Haut-Koenigsbourg, and guided her to the hut where she had found the *Duc*.

"Thank you. . .Mama, thank you!" she said in her heart. "And thank God for looking. . .after me when I was so. . .afraid!"

Chapter Four

Ivona awoke and lay looking in the dim light at the large and beautiful room in which she had been sleeping.

Although she was already half-asleep when she had fallen into bed at three o'clock in the morning, she had still been aware of the magnificence of the Château.

The *Duc*, obviously in pain, had been carried up to his own bedroom, and the *Vicomte* had said to Ivona:

"I expect, Bethune, you are ready for bed, as I am."

"I am very tired," Ivona admitted.

In the carriage on the way back to the Château, the *Vicomte* had been told why she was alone in the woods and, because she was so cold, had found her way to the wood-cutter's hut.

He exclaimed in horror at the idea of her carriage being held up by robbers, but said he had heard of it happening before in some areas of the Vosges Mountains.

"I think you should do something about it," he said to the *Duc*.

Almost before the words had passed his lips, Ivona gave a cry of horror.

"No, no!" she said. "Even to mention that you know about it might draw. . .attention to me. Then my uncle would get me back in his. . clutches. He is my Guardian until I am twenty-one."

"You are right. We must not forget how young you are," the *Vicomte* replied.

Ivona had been amused to notice that when they entered the carriage the *Duc* was carried in first, and his bad leg was propped up for him with cushions so that it stretched out in front of him.

The *Vicomte* entered next and sat beside him, while she as the youngest was expected to sit opposite them with her back to the horses.

She found it amusing to realise that they would have treated her quite differently if they had known she was a woman.

At the same time, it reassured her that they accepted that she was what she looked and had no suspicion that she was in fact of a different sex.

She had noticed too that the men who carried the *Duc* each held under one arm one of the long pieces of wood on which he had been skiing.

He had in fact given the order as they went through the door of the wood-cutter's hut, saying:

"Bring my skis with me. I shall want them again."

"I always said it was a dangerous sport!" the *Vicomte* remarked, but the *Duc* did not reply.

The long pieces of wood were therefore fastened firmly on the roof of the carriage, and the four horses drawing it set off at a very good pace, despite the condition of the road.

Ivona knew that the *Duc*'s Château was about five miles from the *Comte*'s, and she wondered if she would be able to visit what had been her home for four years, then felt it would be a mistake.

She was sure she would be right in thinking that if it was possible, the best thing would be for the *Duc* to convey her to Paris, and once there she could start looking for the de Lesmonts.

"I am sure they will be kind to me," she told herself reassuringly.

At the same time, it was frightening to think of how alone she was in the world, and for the moment with no money.

When she thought of the quite large sum she had left behind at the Château and also the very much larger amount that was in the Bank in her mother's name, she longed for somebody to whom she could confide her problems.

She was certain, however, that it would be a great mistake to take the *Duc* into her confidence.

He seemed kind, but his reputation gave her no assurance that if he learnt she was a woman he would not insist on informing her uncle where she was.

In other words, as far as he was concerned, he would wash his hands of her.

"He has so many lovely ladies in his life that he will certainly not want me as an encumbrance," Ivona reasoned.

Then, as they drove in the carriage, she found it fascinating to listen to the *Duc* and the *Vicomte* talking to each other.

Almost as if they forgot she was there, the *Vicomte* said:

"Frederick is certain that things have speeded up considerably in the last month. There are more troops on the border, more weapons being distributed, and he has learnt from his own special sources that Bismarck is determined upon war."

The *Vicomte* spoke positively and in a low voice, as if he was aware of the secrecy of what he was saying.

Then, as if the *Duc* remembered Ivona, he remarked:

"You have your secrets, Bethune, and we have ours. I do not have to tell you that what you are hearing at this moment must never be repeated to anybody else."

"Of course not!" Ivona cried. "But when you speak of war, do you mean between Germany and France?"

"Exactly!" The *Duc* said wryly.

"I am sorry, Jules," the *Vicomte* interposed, "I should

not have spoken in front of a stranger. In fact, in the darkness I am afraid I had forgotten we were not alone."

"You can trust me, and I have given you my word," Ivona said sharply.

"I am quite certain we can," the *Duc* agreed, "and having heard so much, you might as well hear the rest of it."

"I admit to being curious."

With a fur rug over her knees, Ivona was feeling warm and comfortable. At the same time, although she was tired, she could not help feeling intensely interested in what the *Duc* and his friend were saying.

"The fact is," the *Duc* explained, "that I have received confirmation from somebody in Germany, who is very knowledgeable in these matters, that Bismarck is intent on fighting a war with France."

"He might lose when it comes," the *Vicomte* said.

Although it was dark, Ivona knew the *Duc* shook his head.

"The Germans have been preparing for this for a long time," he replied. "They are better trained and certainly better disciplined than our troops, and when they win they will take over Alsace."

"Are you not being over-pessimistic about that?" the *Vicomte* asked.

"I am facing facts," the *Duc* replied. "The Germans have always coveted Alsace, and although our people are passionately French, inevitably they will pay the price of war by becoming captive beneath the heel of the Prussian jack-boot."

"Oh, I hope you are wrong!" Ivona cried. "I cannot bear to think of their spoiling this beautiful part of France."

"Nor can I," the *Duc* replied, "and that is why I do not intend to stay and watch the horrors which will come."

"You are going away?"

"I am closing my Château, putting my land in the hands of those who will farm it and keep it as best they can, and leaving France."

Ivona was stunned into silence, and the *Vicomte* said:

"I cannot believe you mean what you are saying, Jules, even though I have heard it all before, and I do not think you will enjoy living in England."

"You forget I am half-English," the *Duc* replied.

Ivona started.

She had never heard that of him.

"I have not told you about it before," the *Duc* went on, "but my mother left me a mangificent house, which has been kept in good order for me by one of my English cousins, who is now unfortunately growing old."

He paused as if he was thinking before he continued:

"It stands on a large Estate in Oxfordshire. There is also, I believe, a Hunting-Lodge in Leicestershire and another house at Newmarket, where I will be able to train my horses just as well as at Chantilly."

"When you talked like this a few months ago," the *Vicomte* said in a low voice, "I thought you were only joking or perhaps being hysterical."

"That is something I have never been," the *Duc* interrupted.

But the *Vicomte* went on as if he had not spoken:

"After what Frederick told me today, I have the terrifying feeling that you are about the only man in France who at this moment is seeing clearly what will happen if Bismarck gets his way."

"You are sure. . .quite sure," Ivona asked, "that it will be war?"

"If you have read the newspapers recently," the *Duc* answered, "you must know that Bismarck has encouraged the Prussian Press in a violent campaign against France."

He paused, then continued:

"Ever since he supported Spain against this country, the diplomatic situation has been tense to the point where at any moment the enmity between France and Germany might explode."

"Surely something can be done?" Ivona asked.

She could not bear to think of the Germans, whom she hated, overrunning the country to which she half-belonged, and where she had been so happy since coming to live in Alsace these last four years with her mother and the *Comte*.

"Bethune is right," the *Vicomte* said, "something must be done! Surely you, with your enormous influence, Jules, can make one or two of the members of the Government see sense?"

"I do not believe it is the Government which is at fault," the *Duc* replied, "but somebody quite different."

There was a silence for a moment. Then the *Vicomte* said:

"I presume you are referring to the Empress?"

"Exactly!" the *Duc* replied. "The Empress Eugénie is intriguing with the Minister of War, the *Duc* de Gaumont, and doing everything in her power to attack the Germans openly."

"Even if it is madness?"

"What woman ever considered anything important except the flag-waving, the glory, and the sensationalism of victory?"

"I keep forgetting she is Spanish," the *Vicomte* replied.

"That of course is the main reason for her enmity against the Germans, and she will do anything to strike at them."

It was then that Ivona understood what was being said.

She had listened to the *Comte* telling her mother that although the Empress Eugénie was exceedingly beautiful, she was in fact a stupid woman.

"Her partisanship for her own country," he had said, "and her hatred of Germany have made her blind to everything else. She cannot even see what is best for France."

The *Duc* and the *Vicomte* went on discussing the situation, but for the moment Ivona could think only of herself.

If she reached Paris and there was war, it would be more difficult than it was already for her to find anybody among the de Lesmonts who would protect her from her uncle.

And yet, what was the alternative? To go to the Château and ask the servants to hide her?

If the Germans did march into Alsace, she would be in a very precarious position, and she had a horror of everything she had heard about the Prussians.

She could not have lived in Alsace without realising how hated they were by every Frenchman on the French side of the Rhine.

"What shall I do?" she asked herself desperately, feeling that this was yet another problem, and one for which she was not prepared.

By the time they reached the Château she was too tired to think of anything but an aching desire for sleep.

On what must have been the *Duc's* instructions, a valet brought her a silk nightshirt.

She was grateful to find that there was attached to her bedroom a small bath-room which must at one time have been a powder-closet.

It was therefore possible for her to undress without the valet watching her or attempting to help, and the thick silk of the nightshirt hid her figure as she quickly slipped into bed.

"I understand you've no luggage, *Monsieur*," the valet said, "but I'll press your clothes for you. His Grace has already said that I must try to find something in the Château that will fit you."

"Thank you very much," Ivona managed to reply drowsily.

Then before the valet had left the room she was asleep.

Now she thought how lucky she was to have found help which was so unexpected and which was proving so generous.

"I must be very careful not to let him know who I am," she told herself.

She had very nearly let it slip last night just before they had arrived at the Château, when the *Duc* had said:

"Thank God we are nearly home. I am sure, Bethune, you will be glad to get your head down."

Then, before Ivona could reply, he said:

"I cannot go on being so formal to somebody so much younger than myself. What is your Christian name?"

Because she was so sleepy, the question took her by surprise, and Ivona, forgetting who she was supposed to be, got as far as saying "Ivo. . ." before she managed to bite back the end of the word.

"Ivo," the *Duc* replied. "A delightful old French name which I have not heard used for a long time."

"Nor have I," the *Vicomte* agreed, "although it was one of my father's."

Realising that they had caught her off-guard, Ivona was thankful that "Ivo" had been the name of her grandfather the Ambassador.

Her mother had told her that because she was determined if she had been a boy she should be called after him, there had been quite a fight about it.

"Your father," she said, "was determined that you should be called 'William George,' which are both family names, and only after a great deal of argument did he concede that 'Ivo' could be added to them."

"Then I turned out to be a girl!" Ivona laughed.

"It was a disappointment to your father, but not to me," her mother said. "I am afraid you still had to follow the family tradition. . ."

" 'Harriet Sarah,' " Ivona finished with a little grimace, "but you still managed to tack 'Ivona' onto the end of it."

"And that is what I have always called you," her mother said. "Although your father protested at first, he grew used to it."

"I think it is a lovely name," Ivona said, "and thank you, Mama, for choosing it for me."

She had kissed her mother and they both had laughed.

Without putting it into words, they were well aware that neither "Harriet" nor "Sarah" would have suited her, while "Ivona" undoubtedly did.

"Well, good-night, Ivo," the *Duc* had said as he was carried away to his bedroom.

"Thank you. . . more than I can ever express, Your Grace for your kindness," Ivona had replied.

She had noticed that the valet referred to the *Duc* as *"Monseigneur"* and had felt, although it was a title given to Bishops and members of the Royal Family, that it suited the *Duc*.

She thought he looked like a Prince and that he ruled over his Empire, for that was certainly what it was, like a Monarch.

When she was dressed, wearing the shining boots that had been dried and cleaned after her long walk, she felt a little shy as she went down the stairs.

Because she had been so intent on escaping, it had never struck her how daring it was for a woman to be dressed as a man, and undoubtedly her mother would have been shocked.

It was a strange freedom, which she appreciated, to be able to walk about without the clutter of skirts.

And because she had escaped from the Nun, from the terrors of the Convent, and from dying by her own hand, she felt as if she could jump for joy and join in the song of the birds.

She had heard before she left her bedroom that the *Duc* had been carried downstairs and was now in the Library.

"The Doctor said that His Grace was to stay in bed," the valet had said conversationally, "but *Monseigneur* is a law unto himself, and no-one dares to give him orders!"

Ivona had laughed.

"You make him sound very frightening!"

"I think we're all a little frightened of him, *Monsieur*," the valet had replied. "At the same time, if he asked us to, we would all die for him."

A flunkey dressed in an elaborate and colourful livery led Ivona from the large Hall, decorated with exquisitely carved statues, along a wide corridor.

Here there were paintings that made her long to stop and admire them, but the flunkey opened the door to the Library and she walked in.

The *Duc* was sitting at his desk with a huge pile of

papers in front of him and was giving orders in an
authoritative tone to a secretary who stood beside him,
notebook in hand.

His bandaged ankle was resting on a tapestry-covered
stool.

Otherwise he appeared to be a picture of good health,
and Ivona thought that in the daylight he was even
more handsome than he had appeared the night before.

He was very smartly dressed and might have been on
his way to the Tuileries Palace in Paris.

Woman-like, she was glad that the clothes she had
stolen were as smart and fashionable as those the *Duc*
was wearing.

As she advanced towards him the *Duc* looked at her,
smiled, and said:

"Good-morning, Ivo, I hope you slept well."

"Very well, thank you, *Monseigneur!*"

She saw the *Duc's* eyes twinkle at the way in which
she addressed him but he merely said to his secretary:

"The *Comte* de Bethune will be coming with me to
Paris. In the meantime, having lost his luggage, he
requires clothes."

"I've learnt that already, Your Grace," the secretary
replied.

"Then see that everything is attended to as quickly as
possible. One of the valets can drive into Colmar and
purchase what is immediately necessary. The rest can
of course be obtained in Paris."

"You are very kind," Ivona murmured. "I am afraid I
am being a terrible nuisance."

The *Duc* smiled.

"Only an extra item to be transported, and you will
not be as cumbersome as my statues and my pictures."

"You are taking all of them away?"

"All of them!" the *Duc* said firmly.

Ivona thought for a moment, then she said:

"But surely, even if the Germans beat the French in
a battle, they will not get as far as Paris?"

The *Duc* was silent for a moment, then as his secretary left the room he said:

"You may think it strange, but I was born here in Alsace, and my blood is very sensitive to the 'voices' which you must have heard about and which give us at times clairvoyant powers."

"Of course!" Ivona exclaimed. "Just as Joan of Arc heard 'voices' when she was a child, which told her what she must do, you hear the same."

"I thought perhaps you would understand," the *Duc* said.

Ivona looked at him wide-eyed.

"Why should you think I would do that?"

"The answer to that question is obvious: I use my instinct and it never fails me."

Ivona was intrigued.

Then it struck her that if the *Duc*'s instinct was really perceptive, he might be aware that she was not the boy she was pretending to be.

To change the subject, she walked to the window to stand looking out at the formal gardens and beyond them the other side of the valley, where the snow-covered hills looked very beautiful against the pale sky, from which for the moment the snow-clouds had disappeared.

"How can you leave anything so beautiful?" she asked.

"Whatever happens to Alsace," the *Duc* replied, "it will always remain in its heart French, and even if the Germans take it from France, I know that one day it will be ours again. In the meantime, we shall suffer."

The *Duc* spoke in a voice that sounded as if he was describing what he saw in front of his eyes.

"We shall suffer from the Germans," he went on, "and not once but twice. Then, although it will be long after I am dead, pray God, there will be peace!"

Because the way he spoke moved her and also because she was frightened, Ivona did not say anything.

Then, as if he wished to gainsay such a dismal prophecy, the *Duc* said:

"But now we are still French, we are still free, and if I am proved wrong, then my statues and pictures can come home, and we can all be happy again. However, in the meantime, they will travel."

"To Paris?"

"To England!"

Ivona was so surprised that she turned round to stare at him.

"Do you mean that you are taking all your treasures with you to England?"

"Why not?" the *Duc* answered. "I would not like to go without them any more than I would leave behind my horses."

"You will not like England," she said involuntarily.

The *Duc* raised his eye-brows.

"You speak as if you have been there."

"Yes, I have, and I hated it!"

She knew that was not quite true. She had not hated England itself, the people or the countryside, only her father and the great grey bleak house in which he had instituted a terror as harsh and brutal as anything the Germans could contrive.

"Well, if that is how you feel," the *Duc* said, "I will leave you in Paris, and I am sure you will find somebody to look after you."

Ivona lifted her chin.

"I am quite able to look after myself!"

"I rather doubt that," the *Duc* said quietly. "You have not been very successful so far."

Because she felt it would be ungrateful not to acknowledge how much his kindness meant to her, she said:

"I am very. . .very grateful for the way in which you looked after me. . .last night. . .when I was so cold and. . .lost."

"I told you I do not want your thanks."

"I also thanked God!"

Ivona spoke without thinking, and the *Duc* said with a twist of his lips:

"I stand rebuked."

"No! No! I did not mean that!" Ivona cried. "But of course I said a prayer of gratitude because I was so

fortunate to see the light in the wood-cutter's house,
and you were there."

"It was certainly not a night to be out in the open,"
the *Duc* observed.

"That is something that you might have said to
yourself."

The *Duc* laughed.

"*Touché!*" he said. "But I think you realise by now,
Ivo, that my skiing was an excuse to meet my friend
across the Rhine without anybody being aware of it."

"You make it sound very exciting!"

"It would be if it were not so depressing," the *Duc*
replied. "A long time ago I realised the predicament in
which France was going to find itself, if we were not
very careful, and my friend, although he is of German
nationality, had a mother who was born in Alsace."

"So his sympathies are French," Ivona remarked.

"I think whoever has French blood in him naturally
feels intensely patriotic toward this very beautiful
country."

"Which is something you certainly cannot say either
of Germany or of England," Ivona said.

There was a note in her voice which made the *Duc*
look at her curiously.

"Why do you hate England so ferociously?" he asked.
"Can it be that, like me, you have English blood in
your veins and wish to repudiate it?"

Again he was being uncomfortably perceptive, and
Ivona said quickly:

"I do not wish to talk about myself, but about you,
Monseigneur. Tell me about your horses."

"That is much too obvious a way in which to change
the subject," the *Duc* said, "and, quite frankly, I am
interested in you, Ivo."

"Why?"

"For several reasons," the *Duc* replied evasively.
"But shall I say that, because you came into my life so
unexpectedly and with a most intriguing explanation as
to why you were there, I find you congenial."

"*Merci, Monseigneur!*" Ivona replied a little sarcas-

tically. "I am very happy to be congenial, if that means
you will help me."

"I have always told you I will take you with me to
Paris," the *Duc* said, "and if you tell me whom you
wish to contact as soon as you arrive, I will tell my
Courier, who is going ahead of us, to inform them of
your arrival."

"There is no need for that," Ivona said quickly, "and
actually, I am not entirely certain of their address."

It sounded a rather lame excuse. At the same time,
she did not wish the *Duc* to go poking into her affairs.
He might find out who she was.

She was already relieved that he had not claimed any
knowledge of the de Bethune family, if there was one.

Neither he nor the *Vicomte* had seemed to be familiar with the name, and she could only hope that it had
been a safe choice.

"What do you want to do this morning?" the *Duc*
asked unexpectedly.

"I would like to see your Château," Ivona replied,
"before you pull it to bits."

"Then that is what you shall do," the *Duc* answered.
"Fortunately there is a wheel-chair here, which my
father used in his old age."

* * *

Ivona was entranced by the beauty of the building
and its contents.

The *Duc* was the most eloquent and knowledgeable
guide she could ever have imagined. He seemed to have
a story to tell about each painting or piece of furniture,
or some amusing anecdote which made her laugh, and
she felt she could have gone on listening to him forever.

Then she realised as they went through the rooms
that already what seemed to be a whole army of men
were taking down the paintings behind them, packing
up the furniture so that it would travel without being
scratched, and lifting the beautiful Aubusson carpets
from the floors.

"How can you bear to do this?" she asked suddenly, and the *Duc* said:

"You cannot suppose it gives me any pleasure, but I know that what I am doing is prudent, and one day my sons and grandsons will commend me for listening to what my 'voices' told me was the wise thing to do."

There was nothing Ivona could say to this.

At the same time, she could only pray that his instincts were wrong and that either the Germans would not fight the French or, if they did, the French would win.

The *Vicomte*, who had been out riding, joined them just before luncheon.

"You should have come with me, young man," he said to Ivona, "but you look a bit pale this morning, and I expect you are still exhausted after all the dramatics you encountered yesterday."

"It was not only the robbers who upset me," Ivona said involuntarily.

"No, of course not," he replied in a sympathetic voice, "but your uncle is not likely to find you here."

However, she could not help worrying as to what would happen when the Nun awoke from her dose of laudanum to find that her charge had vanished.

She suspected that she would return to the Château to ask for help from her uncle and aunt in finding her again.

It was not merely a question of Ivona's safety. The important thing would be not to have to return the money which the Convent had been given for taking her into its charge.

"She will go to the Château," Ivona decided, "and I expect Uncle Arthur and Aunt Alice will still be there, doubtless packing up everything that belongs to me to take back to England with them."

Because the Château was so near, she felt herself tremble just in case anyone should realise there was any connection between her and the *Duc*.

Then she reassured herself by realising that it was unthinkable that the Marquis should imagine that she would have walked out of the Hotel and been fortunate enough to find the *Duc* de Sancerre in a wood-cutter's hut.

It was such an absurd story that it was impossible that anybody, even if they were told of it, would believe it to be true.

"I am safe!" Ivona said beneath her breath.

She was sure that, although her uncle might search for her for a day or two, he would soon be ready to believe that she had died in the cold and would go back to England.

"What is worrying you?" the *Duc* asked, and Ivona was aware that she had been silent for a long time.

She was about to say: "Nothing!" then told the truth.

"I am worrying in case when my Tutor informs my uncle that I am missing, he will start looking for me."

"Where is your uncle staying?"

This was a question Ivona had not anticipated.

She thought wildly what she should say, then replied:

"In an Hotel at Holneck, but after he had seen me off with my Tutor, he intended to go to Bordeaux."

It was the first town she could think of which was as far away from Paris as possible.

The *Duc* made no comment. Then he said:

"It is most improbable that your uncle could suspect you are with me, so try to enjoy yourself. I find that expression of anxiety and fear in your eyes perturbs me."

Ivona looked at him in surprise. Then she said:

"You are not to use your. . .Alsatian perception and. . .instincts on me, because it makes me. . .nervous!"

"What do you think they will tell me?" the *Duc* asked quietly.

"Nothing! But the supernatural can sometimes be very creepy."

"It can also be very helpful," the *Duc* corrected, "as you will understand when what I am anticipating comes true."

Again he spoke as if he was looking far into the future, and Ivona thought that he was very different from what she had anticipated when the *Comte* had talked about him.

She had somehow made a special picture of him in which he had seemed excitingly different from other Frenchmen whom she read about in the newspapers or whom the *Comte* had described to her.

He had amused her and her mother by giving them a vivid character-sketch of the Prince Napoleon, who was notorious for his love-affairs and was in some ways feared in Paris.

Because, Ivona thought, he did not wish her mother to feel she was completely out of touch with everything that was gay and amusing in France, he had described many of the great personalities in Paris.

These included the Masters of Literature—Dumas and Flaubert—and once, when he forgot that Ivona was listening, the Emperor himself.

"He is a handsome man," the *Comte* had said. "He has dignity and distinction, but his weakness, and all men have them, is undoubtedly women."

"I suppose every Monarch is pursued as a man," her mother said in her soft voice.

"That is true, but the Emperor does his own pursuing, and any beautiful woman is his prey until she is in his arms, when he very quickly gets bored with her."

"But why?" Ivona's mother had asked in surprise.

"Perhaps it is something in his make-up," the *Comte* replied, "or perhaps there is something wrong with the women who take his fancy. But while he is overwhelmingly generous to them so that they glitter with jewels and have everything that could make for happiness, sooner or later the whole affair is over."

"I find that very sad," Ivona's mother said quietly. "Love should not be lost, but retained by those who find it."

"You are talking about real love," the *Comte* said, "which is a very different thing. I can say, as if I swore it before the Throne of God, that I am far luckier, far more fortunate, than the Emperor, the Prince Napoleon, or the *Duc* de Sancerre will ever be."

The way he spoke had made Ivona feel quite sorry for those three distinguished Frenchmen.

And yet now she asked herself how she could possibly feel sorry for the *Duc* de Sancerre.

The more she was with him, the more she could understand why the servants admitted to being a little frightened of him.

He was magnificent to look at, and there was an authority, a commanding air about him, which made him seem omnipotent.

"As he has everything," she told herself, "he must be happy."

Yet sometimes when he spoke he had a dry note in his voice which she thought had a touch of cynicism about it, and she knew that at other times he spoke mockingly, as if he laughed at life and at himself.

'He is fascinating to women,' she thought, 'and I hope he does not wish to be rid of me too quickly,' at least not until I am safe with Mama's relations.'

Then she remembered that as far as he was concerned she was not a woman but a man, and perhaps his friendships with his own sex lasted longer.

* * *

After a delicious luncheon which forced Ivona to admit, even though she disliked doing so, that the *Duc*'s Chef was even better than the *Comte*'s, the *Vicomte* offered to show Ivona the horses in the stables.

Although she could not ride because she had no habit to wear, it was some solace to be able to admire the magnificent horses which the *Duc* owned, and which were more impressive than any she had ever seen before.

"Jules is fantastic!" the *Vicomte* said admiringly, as they went from stall to stall. "He never allows anybody to buy his horses for him, but always purchases on his own account, and anything he breeds always becomes a champion."

Ivona did not say anything but she was quite certain

that this was another instance of the *Duc* listening to his "voices."

She ran out of adjectives with which to praise the horses. Then as they finished inspecting one stable, they found the *Duc* in his wheel-chair outside in the stableyard.

"I have some new animals I want you to see," he said to the *Vicomte*, "and I have told the grooms to bring them out here to parade them in front of us."

"That is an excellent idea!" the *Vicomte* replied.

He seated himself on the first chair that was brought and sat down beside the *Duc*, and Ivona realised that she had to wait for the next one, which was placed on the other side of him.

The horses came out, one by one, some of them rearing and bucking a little, others walking with a dignity which proclaimed their breeding and the fact that they had been exceptionally well trained.

The *Duc* watched them with a smile.

Then when the parade was over he said:

"Tomorrow they start on their journey to England."

"Are you really going to send them so far?" the *Vicomte* asked. "Supposing after all this fuss, palaver, and expense, the Germans hold out an 'olive-branch' of peace, or the French do?"

"I think you know the answer to both those contingencies," the *Duc* said seriously.

"Damn you! You are making me depressed and uneasy!" the *Vicomte* said. "Tomorrow I shall go to Paris and find out if things are really as black as you are painting them."

"Do not talk to Gaumont, I do not trust him," the *Duc* said, "but call on the Empress. She has a tenderness for you, and she might be more forthcoming with you than she is with me."

"One thing is quite certain," the *Vicomte* said, "if she does not wish to talk politics with you, my friend, it is because she wishes something very different."

The *Duc* smiled, but he made no comment.

Ivona, listening, wondered if there was any woman who would not wish to attract the *Duc*.

She had often thought, from what she had read and what she had heard, that the French were obsessed with love, and she told herself it was something which she had no wish to feel.

She intended never to be married, having resolved never to experience what her mother had suffered at the hands of her father.

She also thought it would be better still never to fall in love, never to become too closely involved with any man.

'Perhaps I can go on for the rest of my life pretending to be a boy,' she thought.

When she looked at herself in the mirror this morning after having dressed, she thought she actually made a very attractive young man.

Because she was so thin, she looked slender and lissom, and if she did not take off her coat there were no tell-tale curves beneath the white linen of her shirt.

Her legs were long and thin, her hips narrow, and she was quite certain that nobody would suspect from her figure that she was anything but a young man.

But her face was rather different.

Her eyes seemed too large to be a young man's, but, although the *Duc* had remarked on it, the *Vicomte* appeared not to have noticed that she looked somewhat fragile to be a boy.

But that, she thought, could be accounted for by the story of her ill health and the fact that when the *Duc* had asked her her age, she had told him she was only just seventeen.

"I suppose you think you are very grown up and very much the 'young man about town,'" he had teased.

"I know you are laughing at me," Ivona had replied, "but I am growing older, and I hope wiser, every minute we are talking to each other."

The *Duc* had laughed as she meant him to do. Then he had said:

"I suppose I looked very much like you when I was

your age, but you will find that in the next two years
you will fill out and become tall and strong. Then you
can certainly justify telling yourself you are an excellent
example of the superior and dominant sex."

"I shall certainly try to do that," Ivona had answered,
"and once this tiresome chest of mine has cleared up, I
am certain that, as you say, I shall grow very much
stronger."

She thought the *Duc* had accepted this, and she was
quite certain he was not in the least suspicious, although she might look somewhat feminine, about her
being one of what he described as the "superior sex."

She had taken the precaution when she was in her
bath-room to cut her hair a little shorter and tidy up the
rough pieces that had been left after she had cut it off in
such a hurry.

She found herself thinking with a smile that one day,
and she hoped it would be a long time ahead, somebody tidying the young man's bedroom at the Hotel
would find a Nun's robe behind the wardrobe and the
long tresses of fair, red-tipped hair bundled up with it.

Then with a little tremble of fear she knew, although
she had not thought of it before, that when the valet
found that his Master's clothes had vanished, they would
know who had taken them.

'The sooner I get away from here, the better!' she
thought.

But for the moment she had to wait for the *Duc*
because she could not travel without any money.

After inspecting the horses they went back to the
Château and into the Library, where the *Duc* talked of
some books he had there which were to be packed up.

The workmen had been instructed to start the next
day.

"Have you a Library in your house in England big
enough to take all these?" Ivona asked.

"The strange thing is," the *Duc* replied, "that I find it
difficult to remember! I have only visited Beckhampton
Priory three times in my life: once when I was only a
boy and I went to stay there with my mother; then with

my grandfather, who was the Earl of Beckhampton, and
I was more interested in his horses than in the contents
of his house."

"Were his horses very fine?" Ivona enquired.

"Not as fine as mine," the *Duc* asserted, "but quite
impressive!"

"Go on," Ivona prompted.

"The third time was after my mother had died. Since
both her brothers had been killed, the house was left to
her with the Estate."

"That seems strange," Ivona remarked without thinking,
"for usually in England there are cousins to inherit the
title."

"I see you are well read!" the *Duc* said drily. "In fact,
one of my cousins did come into the title, and it is now
his son's."

"And the house and the Estate?" Ivona enquired.

"They belonged to my grandfather, who bought them
as he disliked the family house in Staffordshire because he considered it too far away from London."

"Now I understand," Ivona said. "So he left it to his
daughter, who left it to you."

"Exactly!" the *Duc* agreed. "So I am very fortunate in
having waiting for me in England very much the same
sort of possessions I have at the moment in France."

He paused to add:

"However, they do not, I am quite certain, contain
the same sort of treasures that I and my father have
collected here and our ancestors before us."

Ivona laughed.

"I imagine when you arrive in England the English
will think you are a god arriving from another Planet
and be astounded both by you and by your possessions,
and the way you have descended on them unexpectedly."

"How do you know the English will feel like that?"
the *Duc* asked.

Ivona thought she had been indiscreet, and she replied quickly:

"As I told you, I have been to England, and found it
very stolid and unimaginative, and often cruel."

She thought of her father as she spoke, and her eyes darkened and a little shiver went through her.

She was not aware that the *Duc* was watching her.

Then he bent toward her and said very quietly:

"Who has hurt you? And why are you afraid?"

Chapter Five

When Ivona went to bed the following night she thought she had never spent a day which had been more fun.

The *Vicomte* had left early in the morning for Paris and she had been alone with the *Duc*.

In the morning, because he was expecting the Doctor, they inspected more treasures in the Château, and he told her such fascinating stories of his ancestors that she wished he would write them down and put them in a book.

She suggested that this was what he should do, and he said:

"It is a pity I am going to England, otherwise I might have offered you a job as my Curator."

For a moment Ivona played with the possibility of this happening if she went to England with the *Duc*.

Then she knew she would be far too afraid even to be in the same country as her uncle.

She thought that by this time he would have given up the search for her and perhaps returned home, but she could not be sure of anything.

The *Duc* had never mentioned the *Comte* as being one of his near-neighbours, and she was far too nervous to ask if he knew of him or his Château.

After luncheon the *Duc* announced that although it still hurt him to walk and the Doctor had said he must rest his leg for another day or so, he had every intention of riding.

For a moment Ivona's spirits dropped, thinking she must be left behind. Then he said with a smile:

"If you look in your bedroom I think you will find something which will enable you to keep me company."

Sure enough, the *Duc*'s valet had brought out of some attic, or wherever they had been kept, breeches and riding-coats which the *Duc* had worn as a young boy.

There was a choice, and she found that the smallest of them fitted her almost perfectly.

Riding-boots were more difficult, but one pair, although a little large, were quite comfortable, and as she ran downstairs to find the *Duc* waiting for her in the Hall, she hoped he would think that she looked smart enough to accompany him.

He as usual was looking magnificent, and although he said that it had hurt his ankle to pull on his boot, he did not appear now as if he was suffering any pain.

It was a strange feeling to be riding astride rather than side-saddle, and when they first set off Ivona was tense in case she should do something stupid and the *Duc* would think she was not a good rider.

Her father had always possessed excellent horses, and because her mother was not very fond of riding she had regularly accompanied him since she had been very small.

She was therefore very much at home in the saddle, and she had loved riding with the *Comte* when he was at the Château and with a groom when he was not there.

The horse the *Duc* had chosen for her was spirited but well trained, and after they had gone a little distance he said:

"I thought you would be a good rider!"

"I am glad your intuition was right in this instance," Ivona replied.

"I suppose it is a compliment you appreciate," he said drily.

She found herself wondering what sort of compliments he would pay her if he knew she was a woman, but told herself that that was something she would never know.

They rode over the snow-covered fields that were beginning to thaw as it had not snowed the day before and the sun had been hot.

Looking over the valley and up toward the mountains, Ivona thought nothing could be more beautiful.

"How can you leave this?" she asked impulsively. "Perhaps you should stay and help to retain it."

"I have thought of that," the *Duc* replied seriously. "The Generals commanding our Armies are quite convinced that they are equal to, if not better than, the Germans in efficiency."

"And you think differently?"

"I know that the Germans have better artillery, more up-to-date weapons, and many more professional, highly trained soldiers."

Ivona was sure he had learnt this from his friend Frederick, and she said:

"I prayed last night that you would be wrong, and I think I hate. . .your. . .'voices'!"

"I can understand your feeling like that," the *Duc* said quietly, "but before very long you will know I am right."

As if the idea upset him, he spurred his horse to a gallop and went ahead of her, and she had difficulty in keeping up with him.

However, when they returned to the Château his mood had changed, and he talked to her with a wit and intelligence which made her listen wide-eyed to everything he said.

Although the *Comte* had been well read and also an intelligent man, he had been so obsessed by her mother that she had never had a chance to duel with him in words.

In fact, everything he had said was tinged with love.

The *Duc*, however, talked to Ivona as if she were his equal and his contemporary, and when they went up to bed she told herself that that was the relationship she would always like to have with a man, because then she need never be afraid.

She had already told the valet who looked after her that she liked to be alone.

After he had taken away her evening-coat, which also had been one of the *Duc's* when he was young, she dismissed him and took off the rest of her clothes very slowly.

Then she put on the silk nightshirt that had been left for her.

It was too long and she had to lift it up when she walked. In fact, it was so voluminous that it gave no hint of her figure, and she did not feel nervous of the valet calling her in the morning.

When she looked at herself in the mirror before she got into bed, she thought perhaps it would be a pity when she reached Paris to have to revert to being a woman again.

She was certain that this would mean she would be paid fulsome compliments by any Frenchman to whom she was introduced.

She knew she had no wish to hear them, and she thought how much more pleasant life could be if she were able to converse with other men on serious subjects, as she could with the *Duc*.

There were so many interesting topics that were ignored when one was a woman: politics, the impending war, even the Art that she longed to see in Paris.

She was sure that any conversation about Art would somehow be twisted, if she was herself, into discussions or expressions of love rather than of artistic merit.

"I will stay as a man," she told herself definitely.

But she knew it was impossible because she did not have any money, and she was hoping that her de Lesmont relations would provide for her.

She sat thinking for some time in front of the mirror.

She began to grow cold despite the fact that the Château was kept beautifully warm with the pretty tiled stoves which burned in every room.

She rose to her feet and blew out the candles on the dressing-table, leaving only one alight beside her bed.

As she did so, she heard the jingle of horses' bridles outside and thought it strange.

It was impossible to imagine that anybody was calling at this hour of the night. At the same time, if they did, she would not hear wheels because of the snow.

Because she was curious, she pulled aside one of the heavy blue brocade curtains and opened the casement.

Two of the windows in the room were shuttered at night, but she had told the maids to leave one window unshuttered because first thing in the morning she liked to look out and breathe the fresh air.

Now she felt the sharpness of the frost on her cheeks and knew it was a mistake to let it get into her throat.

Then as she looked down she saw that there was a carriage outside, drawn by four horses, with two men on the box.

The footman alighted to open the door of the carriage, and as she watched she saw a man alight, wearing a top-hat, followed by two other men.

There was the light of the carriage-lamps, and also the moon, which had guided Ivona when she had escaped from the Hotel, was high in the sky.

It was fuller and even brighter than it had been when it helped her to find her way to the wood-cutter's hut.

Because she was so surprised at visitors calling at this late hour, after the *Duc* had retired, she did not draw back and close the window.

Despite the cold, she leant forward to watch them climb the steps, which were a little to the right of her window, and ring the front-door bell.

As they waited, the man who had stepped out first looked up at the house as if he was appraising it, and she had a glimpse of his face.

Then she felt as if her heart stopped beating and her bare feet were frozen to the floor.

It was her uncle who stood there, and she realised now that with him were two *Gendarmes*.

* * *

The *Duc*, having got into bed, knew—and it annoyed him—that his sprained ankle was aching.

He was aware that it was against the Doctor's instructions that he had used it, but he had wanted to ride, and above anything else he disliked not taking enough exercise.

Now he thought, with one of his twisted smiles, that he was paying for his enjoyment and there was no use complaining.

However, he was glad to have his leg stretched out in front of him and was certain that after a night's rest the pain would have gone.

Because it was very early for him to retire, he had brought with him the work he would otherwise have done downstairs at his desk.

He had instructed his valet to arrange a number of cushions behind his back, and he had a large silver candelabrum with six candles burning in it at his side.

Before he picked up the papers, a number of which were lists of his paintings and furniture which he was removing to England, he looked round his room and thought how much he would regret leaving it.

In the whole Château, in which every room was outstanding and a connoisseur's dream, the *Duc's* bedroom, which had been used by a number of his ancestors, was perhaps the most artistic.

The ceiling was a masterpiece that had been acclaimed as the finest work Verrio had ever done.

In the walls of white and gold-leaf were set panels of the finest silk brocade from Lyons, and the paintings he had specially chosen to hang there glowed like jewels.

It was a room to dream in, the *Duc* often thought, a room in which he had often felt that his "voices" spoke to him more clearly than in any other.

He could not bear to think of Germans, with their lack of spirituality, occupying it.

And yet he knew they would take over Alsace, and there was nothing he or any other Frenchman who loved the Province could do to stop them.

But thoughts of the future upset him, and the *Duc* deliberately picked up his papers, starting with one on which was listed his paintings and the names of the artists who had painted them.

Then, instead of seeing them, in his mind's eye he found Ivona's face intruding itself on his thoughts.

Suddenly, as if his imagination had conjured her up, his door was flung open.

She burst into the room, pushing the door to behind her, and as the *Duc* stared at her in astonishment, she said in a voice vibrant with fear:

"Help me. . .please help me. . .my uncle is here. . .and has with him two. . .*Gendarmes!* They have. . .come to take me. . .away!"

Because she was trembling with fear, her words were almost incoherent, but the *Duc* could hear the terror in them.

He did not speak but merely turned on his side and pulled back the sheets and blankets on the huge bed.

As if she understood, Ivona, like a small animal finding sanctuary below ground, slipped into the bed, which was covered with a white fur-rug.

The *Duc* then threw the papers which had been placed in a neat pile beside him over where Ivona was hiding and went on reading what he held in his hand.

It was only a few minutes later when there was a knock on the door.

When it opened, his valet, Gascoigne, who had been with him for many years, said in a voice which held a note of warning in it:

"A gentleman has called, *Monseigneur*, who demands to see you!"

The *Duc* raised his head without hurry to ask:

"Demands?"

"*Oui, Monseigneur.*"

Before the valet had finished speaking, the Marquis of Morecombe walked into the room, and the *Duc* saw that pausing in the doorway behind him were two *Gendarmes*.

The *Duc* looked at the newcomer in a manner which would have made most men cringe, before he said:

"I am not receiving at this hour, *Monsieur*."

"I am aware of that," the Marquis replied.

His French was fluent, but he spoke with an excruciatingly bad accent as he went on:

"I am the Marquis of Morecombe, and I have learnt that Your Grace has been deceived into harbouring a criminal!"

The *Duc* stared at him as if in astonishment before he said:

"I think, My Lord, you have been misinformed."

"I am told," the Marquis replied harshly, "that you have staying with you a young man who pretends to be the *Comte* de Bethune. He is in fact my niece, Lady Ivona Combe, who has stolen the garments she is wearing, besides committing a number of other offences."

The Marquis spoke impressively in the resonant tones he used in Church when he was denouncing sinners.

The *Duc* was silent for a moment.

Then unexpectedly he put back his head and laughed.

The sound seemed to ring out through the bedroom, a sound of natural, undisguised amusement.

As the Marquis stared at him incredulously, the *Duc* said:

"Forgive me, but this is a joke too good to miss, that you should believe that I, with my reputation, should not recognise a member of the 'Fair Sex' whatever she was wearing!"

"Your levity is misplaced, Your Grace!" the Marquis replied. "I assure you I am not speaking idly when I tell you that Lady Ivona was being taken to a Convent where she would have been compelled to do penance both for her own sins and for the wickedness committed by her mother. But she escaped when a fall of snow blocked the road."

"You say this girl was being taken to a Convent?" the *Duc* remarked conversationally.

"To the Convent at Haut-Koenigsbourg," the Marquis replied, "where the strict discipline would have, with God's help, prevented her from behaving in such an unseemly way in the future!"

"And you thought that was the right sort of place to send your niece?" the *Duc* asked.

"It was the only place suitable for the depravity with which she had been contaminated in living with her mother, whose sinful liaison with the *Comte* de Gambois must have been known to Your Grace, since you live in the same neighbourhood."

"Now I am aware of whom you are speaking," the *Duc* said. "But surely your niece's punishment for what you call her mother's wickedness is somewhat severe?"

"The Bible clearly says that 'the sins of the fathers shall be visited upon the children,' " the Marquis thundered, "and she will also be punished, and very severely, for stealing, and for drugging the Nun who was escorting her."

"A long list of crimes!" the *Duc* remarked mockingly. "You have made me curious about this young Electra, or is it one of the Borgias that she resembles?"

There was no doubt that he was amused, and the Marquis said sharply:

"You may think it a laughing matter, Your Grace, but I must require you in the name of the law to hand over my Ward. I promise you that she will be no more trouble to you or to anybody else in the future."

"Even if I wished to oblige you," the *Duc* answered, "it would be impossible."

"What do you mean—impossible?" the Marquis asked angrily.

"If you are referring to the young man I know as the *Comte* de Bethune, who you tell me is an imposter, he has already left."

"Left?"

The word was a shout, and the *Duc* replied:

"My friend, the *Vicomte* de Valmont, departed early

this morning for Colmar, where he was taking the train to Paris. The *Comte* de Bethune went with him."

The *Duc* spoke in a manner which made the Marquis feel and resent that he was scoring a point over him.

It was obvious from the darkness of his eyes and the colour creeping up his heavy, gloomy countenance that his temper was rising.

"I do not believe it!" he said furiously. "My informant told me positively that Lady Ivona was here in your Château."

"Your informant," the *Duc* replied blithely, "was misinformed!"

"I insist you allow these Policemen to search the place."

The *Duc* looked at the *Gendarmes* standing awkwardly in the doorway as if he saw them for the first time.

Then he spoke to them authoritatively and so quickly that it was difficult for the Marquis to follow exactly what he was saying to them.

The *Gendarmes*, looking even more uncomfortable than before, bowed and said respectfully:

"Naturally we accept your word, *Monsieur le Duc*. Please pardon our intrusion. We are only acting on orders from our Superior."

"Then inform your Superior what I have said," the *Duc* replied. "Tell him I commend your discretion and accept your apology for bursting into the privacy of my bedroom."

There was a sharp edge to his voice on the last words, which made the two *Gendarmes* take several paces back into the corridor.

Then the *Duc* turned to the Marquis.

"Good-night, My Lord," he said. "I consider your intrusion extremely discourteous, if not an insult! My servant will show you out."

"I do not. . ." the Marquis began.

The *Duc* interrupted him.

"I said 'good-night,' My Lord!"

There was something so dictatorial and intimidating

in the way he spoke that the Marquis was defeated and
he knew it.

With an ill grace and scowling with fury, he walked
from the room, while Gascoigne, who had been standing
just inside the room all the time the interchange was
taking place, moved after him.

Only when he was about to shut the door behind him
did the *Duc* say so that only he could hear:

"Do not allow the Marquis to question anybody, and
find out from the *Gendarmes* from whom they had their
information."

Gascoigne did not speak, but only nodded and followed the Marquis down the stairs.

He had been with the *Duc* for many years and had
accompanied him on many secret escapades, including
the most recent, in which His Grace had obtained
information from Germany.

The *Duc* knew that he would not fail him.

There had been many times in his life when he had
found an accomplice as reliable and faithful as Gascoigne
very useful.

Now the room was very quiet, but the *Duc* did not
speak and Ivona did not move.

Only when perhaps three minutes had passed did the
Duc say quietly:

"I think now it is safe for you to come out."

He put out his hand as he spoke and pulled aside the
sheets and blankets as he had done before to show her
the hiding-place.

Slowly, as if she was still afraid, Ivona moved up the
bed until she was facing him.

Her eyes, dark with fear, seemed to fill her whole
face, which was very white, and the red on her curls
caught the light from the candles.

For a moment she only looked at him.

Then she said in a voice that was barely audible:

"Are you. . .very angry that I have. . .deceived you?"

The *Duc* smiled.

"I was not deceived!"

"You mean. . .you knew?"

"Of course! As I said to your uncle, you can hardly expect anybody with my reputation to be so obtuse."

"It. . .it was the. . .only way I could. . .escape."

"I can understand that, and now I want you to tell me the whole story from the very beginning."

Ivona gave a little sigh.

Then, as if she did not feel there was anything to make her embarrassed in being beside the *Duc* in the same bed, she sat back against the pillows as he was doing, and stared with unseeing eyes in front of her.

She clasped her fingers together amongst the papers he had thrown over the bed, and she was trembling as she began:

"I am sure. . .now that when he. . .finds I am not in Paris he will still. . .go on looking for me."

"I want to hear everything," the *Duc* said quietly. "Why did you come to France with your mother and live with the *Comte* de Gambois?"

"Did you know Mama was there?"

"I heard about her," the *Duc* answered. "The whole of Alsace was talking about the very beautiful lady the *Comte* had installed in his Château which had been closed for many years."

"It was the one. . .safe place where we could. . .hide."

"From your father?"

"Y-yes."

"Why?"

Hesitatingly, finding it somehow agonising to live over again the horrors she had experienced, she told the *Duc* how her father had beaten her mother, then her.

As she talked, she even forgot that the *Duc* was listening. It all seemed to be happening again, so that her voice vibrated with pain.

Her fingers clasped one another until they were bloodless, and she was trembling uncontrollably.

Then as she told the *Duc* how after they had met the *Comte* at her grandfather's funeral in Paris, he had been waiting for them in Calais, her tone changed.

As she described the happiness they had found in the Château, the sunshine came back into her voice.

"We were very happy," she said, "and that was when I grew to love Alsace."

She paused before, like a cloud coming over the sun, she told of the accident which had killed her mother and the *Comte*.

Then she told of how, when she had not expected it, her uncle had arrived at the Château.

Now fear seemed to vibrate from her as she related how the Nun had arrived to take her to the Convent at Haut-Koenigsbourg and how she had overheard her aunt suggesting that she should be flogged.

"I could not bear it. . .I could not bear it again," she whispered, "and I. . .knew I must. . .kill myself!"

"Kill yourself?" the *Duc* questioned.

It was the first time he had spoken since she had begun her story.

"There was. . .nothing else I. . .could do," Ivona replied, "but the. . .difficulty was. . .how to do it."

She went on to tell him how she thought it had been the answer to her prayers when she remembered that her aunt took laudanum to make her sleep.

She explained how she had taken the bottle and carried it with her, with the intention of swallowing it at the first opportunity.

When the carriage was held up by the road being blocked by snow and they had therefore been forced to stay at the Hotel, she relived that last dinner when she had noticed the smart young man who was about her size at the next table.

She had asked for the coffee and only when she was just about to drink the laudanum herself had the idea occurred to her of drugging the Nun instead.

"You know the rest," Ivona went on. "I put on the young man's clothes, climbed out the window of the Hotel, and. . .walked and walked until I. . .found you."

"I can only feel certain that your Guardian Angel, or whoever it is you pray to, brought you to the wood-cutter's hut," the *Duc* said.

"That is what I thought," Ivona answered, "and if you

had turned into St. Michael and the whole Heavenly Host, I would not have been surprised!"

The *Duc* laughed.

"Fate was certainly on your side. But now, what are we going to do about your uncle?"

"Help me so that he. . .cannot find me."

"I will do my best," the *Duc* answered, "but you realise that if he is determined in his search for you, it will not be easy to foil him."

Ivona gave a little cry of fear.

"Please. . .please. . .you must help me. . .there is nobody in the world. . .except you!"

"That is what I was thinking."

"I am. . .sorry to be an encumbrance. . .and a trouble," she said humbly, "but. . .as you know. . .I have. . .no money."

"That is immaterial," the *Duc* replied, "but I have a feeling that your uncle is determined to track you down as if you were a wild animal, and he will not give up easily."

"He feels like that because he. . .wanted me to be punished. He hated Mama, and therefore he would like to watch me flogged to death. . .or burning in all the. . .fires of Hell!"

There was a frantic note in her voice.

The *Duc* started to put out his hand towards her, then checked himself.

"I do not think you are exaggerating the danger you are in," he said, "but I have a solution to your problem."

"What. . .is it?"

There was a little pause before the *Duc* said very quietly:

"That you should be married!"

Ivona turned her face to look at him in sheer astonishment. Then she said:

"How can you suggest. . .anything so. . .horrible?"

"I am sorry you should feel like that," the *Duc* said, "because if you were married, your uncle could not touch you."

"I. . .I have decided I will. . .never marry anbody!" Ivona said passionately.

Then, as if she felt she was being over-dramatic, she added:

"Besides. . .I do not know any men. . .there is nobody I could. . .marry."

"You know me."

For a moment Ivona was so still that she could not even breathe.

Then she looked at him again to ask:

"Are you. . .really suggesting that I should. . .marry you?"

"As you say, you do not know any other men," the *Duc* replied.

"Are you. . .serious?"

"Yes."

"But. . .how can you think of anything. . .so absurd. . . so unsuitable from. . .your point of view?"

"That is for me to decide. I have to be married sometime."

He spoke drily, in his usual somewhat cynical manner, and it came to Ivona's mind that in France marriages were always arranged by the families concerned.

"I think you are. . .laughing at me," she said. "How could your family. . .accept me as the. . .wife of the *Duc* de Sancerre?"

"I see no difficulty about that aspect of it," the *Duc* said in what was almost a tired voice. "You are the daughter of an English nobleman, your mother comes from a very distinguished French family, and as you tell me your uncle made you sign a Will in his favour, you obviously have enough money to constitute, if nothing else, an acceptable dowry."

Ivona was silent. Then she said, as if she spoke to herself:

"How can I. . .marry anybody. . .or trust any man, after the way my father treated my mother?"

"All men do not behave like your father. He obviously became insane after his accident."

Ivona was silent again. Then she said:

"I suppose I should be. . .very honoured that you

should even. . .suggest that I should become your wife. . .but it is. . .wrong!"

"Why?"

"Because you are so important. . .and. . ."

She paused, not knowing quite how to put what she was thinking into words, and the *Duc* said:

". . .and I have a reputation for being involved with many beautiful women! But as you obviously would not feel jealous, why should that perturb you?"

Ivona could not find an answer to this and could only think how happy her mother had been with the *Comte*, and how overwhelmingly they had loved each other.

But she had been his mistress, not his wife, and if the *Comtesse* had known about her mother, perhaps it had not upset her.

As if once again the *Duc* was following her thoughts, he said:

"Of course, if you were in love with me, that would make things different. As it is, the one obstacle I can see is that you might consider me much too old for you."

"That has nothing to do with it," Ivona replied. "I think you are magnificent. . .when I went to bed tonight I thought that talking to you as we had today was the most. . .exciting and interesting thing I have ever done in my whole life!"

She paused before she asked:

"Could I not. . .just stay with you as I am. . .I prefer being a man. . .to a woman."

"I can see a great many difficulties about that," the *Duc* said, "beside the fact that your uncle has already penetrated your disguise."

As if she had forgotten that, Ivona made a little sound that was like a cry and said:

"If he finds me again. . .I shall have to die. . .or else go into the. . .Convent!"

"Exactly!" the *Duc* agreed. "So the only alternative is to marry me, even though you may think it unpleasant."

"Of course I think nothing of the sort!" Ivona said almost crossly. "I was thinking of you."

"Then think of yourself!"

There was silence. Then she said in a very small voice which he could barely hear:

"Suppose. . .supposing I. . .tempt you?"

She was thinking that she had realised now that every time her father thought her mother tempted him by her beauty, he had beaten her.

"That is impossible," the *Duc* said firmly.

"Why?"

"Because if we were married, I should be tempting you."

Ivona once again looked at him in surprise, and he said:

"I thought you were well read. You must be aware that the Devil in the form of the serpent tempted Eve."

Ivona thought this over for a moment. Then she said:

"But Adam said: 'The woman gave me of the tree, and I did eat.' "

The *Duc* laughed.

"That was his excuse for being disobedient, but I assure you, Ivona, that I am the tempter, not the tempted, the hunter, not the hunted, in anything that concerns love."

It flashed through Ivona's mind that this was undoubtedly the truth.

She could not imagine him being anything but dominant and invariably taking the initiative.

At the same time, she was still afraid.

The *Duc* put out his hand, palm upwards, toward her, saying:

"Give me your hand."

Ivona did as he told her and he could feel her fingers trembling.

His hand closed over hers. Then he said:

"Because we are both Catholics, I swear to you on my immortal soul, which I believe I possess, that I will never ill-treat you physically any more than I would ill-treat my horses or anything which I own."

There was a solemn note in his voice which she had never heard before.

Then, as if he left her free to make her own decision, he released her hand.

There was a little pause before Ivona said:

"If you are. . .quite certain that is what you wish to do. . .I would feel. . .safe if I. . .were married to you."

For a moment there was silence. Then the *Duc* said in a very different voice:

"Very well, we will now make plans, and because I think your uncle is a very real menace, we will be married tomorrow!"

Ivona did not speak, but she drew in her breath.

"First," the *Duc* said, "we must find you some clothes, for I do not think my Chaplain, intelligent though he may be, would appreciate my marrying you dressed in the clothes you have stolen or in what you are wearing now!"

Ivona gave a little chuckle, and he went on:

"Go to bed, Ivona, and leave everything to me. I promise you that however difficult and unpleasant you may find me as a husband, I am infinitely preferable to the Mother Superior of the Convent at Haut-Koenigs-bourg!"

"I know that," Ivona agreed, "and I want to thank you."

"That would bore me!" the *Duc* said quickly. "Now, go to bed, and sleep soundly, being certain that your uncle is off on a 'wild goose chase' to Paris!"

Ivona got out of the bed.

Only as she was standing on the floor did she suddenly feel embarrassed because her feet were bare and she was wearing nothing but one of the *Duc's* silk nightshirts.

However, as if having solved her problem the *Duc* was no longer concerned with her, he was looking down at the papers he had strewn over the bed-cover and did not glance at her as she walked across the room toward the door.

As she opened it she said:

"Good-night, *Monseigneur*, and thank you. . .thank you. . .for being so. . .wonderful!"

"Good-night, Ivona!" the *Duc* replied.

As she walked down the corridor she was aware that the *Duc* was so quickly absorbed in his papers again that he had not even looked up at her as he spoke.

*   *   *

The next morning Ivona awoke with an irrepressible feeling of happiness.

For the first time, she knew she was not afraid that her uncle would appear unexpectedly during the day, or that inadvertently she would give herself away to the *Duc*.

Instead, when she went down the stairs, thinking perhaps she was later than he expected, she felt a little shy, being aware that although she was wearing trousers, the *Duc* knew she was a woman.

However, his attitude toward her was exactly the same as it had been yesterday and the day before that.

He was looking extremely handsome, and as she entered the Library, where she expected to find him, he said:

"Good-morning, Ivona! As soon as you are ready we are driving over to the *Comte's* Château "

"Is that. . .safe?" Ivona asked.

"One of my servants has just returned from there," the *Duc* answered, "and tells me that your uncle and his wife left at half-past-six this morning to drive to Colmar to catch the train to Paris."

"They are going to Paris!"

"To look for you," the *Duc* replied.

She sighed.

"That means I cannot go and search for Mama's relatives, or stay in your house in the Champs Élysées."

"But that is where you will stay," the *Duc* said, "as the *Duchesse* de Sancerre, so there is nothing your uncle can do about it."

He saw the light in her eyes and went on:

"We will go now to what has been your home for the

last few years, and find what your uncle, after his accusation against you of thieving, has taken away with him."

Ivona remembered how she had been sure her aunt would make some excuses to her own conscience for taking her expensive clothes and her fur-coat back to England.

When she and the *Duc* arrived at the Château and were greeted warmly by the servants, she went up to her bedroom to find, as she expected, that the wardrobes were empty.

Only her silk and lace underclothes were left behind, because her aunt thought them "sinful," but fortunately none of her mother's things had been touched.

She therefore knew with an irrepressible gladness, because she wanted to please the *Duc*, that the beautiful gowns the *Comte* had sent from Paris just before he and her mother had been killed were all available for her.

She was about the same size, and she knew that if she was wearing her mother's clothes, she would feel close to her, as if she were still alive.

This made her remember her mother's jewellery, and when she questioned the elderly manservant, she found that as it had been put in the safe, it was still there.

"*Monsieur le Marquis* demanded the key, M'mselle," the servant said, "but I told him I did not have it in my keeping, and although he searched he could not find it."

"That was splendid of you!" Ivona cried.

Although the few things she had left in her bedroom had vanished, she found in the safe not only her mother's jewels but also the large amount of money she kept there.

Ivona felt that this would enable her to feel less completely dependent on the *Duc*, and she told herself that when they reached Paris she would buy him a present.

For the moment, however, she was concerned with changing from her male attire into something feminine which would make her look more respectable, and she went upstairs.

There, the housemaids who had loved her mother began fussing round her, considerably shocked at her trousers and by the fact that she had cut her hair.

"It was the only way I could escape from the Nun," she told them, "and *Monsieur le Duc* saved me from being taken to the Convent at Haut-Koenigsbourg."

"It is wrong and wicked that you should be taken anywhere where life is so harsh!" one of the older housemaids exclaimed. "After you had left, we all cried for you, *M'mselle*."

"Thank you," Ivona replied, "but now I am very happy."

Then she added:

"I am to be married to *Monsieur le Duc!*"

For a moment they could hardly believe it.

Then they flung up their hands in delight and wished her every blessing and a large family of children.

Ivona thought that was very unlikely, but she did not wish to disillusion them.

Instead, she said that she must hurry and change as the *Duc* was ashamed that she should be seen dressed as a man.

"I do not know what your mother, God rest her soul, would say if she saw you, *M'mselle*," one of the housemaids exclaimed. "It is very immodest for a lady to show her ankles, let alone her legs!"

"It does not matter now that I am free," Ivona replied.

Then she remembered with a little quiver of fear that when she was married, as she had never intended to be, she would not be free.

But once again she could hear the note of sincerity in the *Duc*'s voice when he had vowed that he would never hurt her.

"He will not break his word," she told herself reassuringly.

At the same time, because the idea of being anybody's wife still scared her, she could not repress a little tremor of fear.

Chapter Six

As the train moved out of Colmar Station, Ivona knew that the *Duc* was saying good-bye to Alsace.

He had obviously been deeply moved by his last sight of the great Château where so many rooms were already dismantled.

Also, as he said good-bye to those servants who would not be following them to Paris, Ivona knew instinctively how sadly he was feeling the moment of parting.

Although he had said nothing to them about his fears of the German invasion, she was certain they were aware of it, as was everybody in Alsace, and the fact that the *Duc* was taking away so many of his belongings told its own story.

They were travelling in a comfort she had never known before, for the *Duc* had his own private carriage attached to the train.

It was, she saw at first glance, very comfortable with two bedrooms, a Drawing-Room, and a Pantry where the servants, who travelled in another coach, could dish up and serve the food they were to eat on the journey.

She was aware that the Guard's Van which was attached to this particular train was filled to overflowing with their luggage.

She herself had quite a lot, because she had packed up at the Château everything that had belonged to her mother, and her clothes alone had filled a great number of leather trunks.

She was at the moment wearing one of her mother's gowns, which made her feel more like a married woman than if she had been wearing one of her own.

They had been married early this morning in the Chapel attached to the Château by the *Duc's* own private Chaplain, who also officiated at the Church in the village.

Because she thought she must remember her Wedding-Day as something very special, Ivona had searched through her mother's clothes for an appropriate gown.

The only one which was white was a very elaborate creation by Frederick Worth in white and silver, which she knew was a Ball-gown.

"I do not think I could wear that," she said to herself, but the housemaid who was with her exclaimed:

"But of course, *M'mselle!* It is exactly what you should wear! And there is a lace stole amongst *Madame's* things which would make a perfect wedding-veil!"

Ivona remembered that on one occasion when he arrived from Paris the *Comte* had brought her mother a miscellaneous collection of lace.

"I saw it being sold at an exhibition of French and Belgian industries," he had said, "and because it was so fragile and beautiful, it reminded me of you, my darling."

"You flatter me," her mother had said as she kissed him.

Afterwards, Ivona had sorted through the lace and knew that the *Comte* had been right when he said it was beautiful.

The long stole, as the housemaid had said, made her a very lovely veil, and she wore it over her head but not over her face, held in place by a wreath of white orchids which came from the greenhouses in the garden.

She also carried a bouquet of the same flowers.

When she went downstairs to where the *Duc* was waiting for her in the Hall, she thought that he would not have been ashamed of his bride even if they were being married in Notre Dame.

However, he did not say anything as he offered her his arm, and she felt a little disappointed that he did not compliment her on her appearance, as she felt any other Frenchman would have done.

Then she told herself that theirs was only a marriage of convenience, especially as far as she was concerned.

'Once I am his wife, I shall be safe from Uncle Arthur,' she thought.

She hoped that the *Duc* would feel he was getting as good a bargain as she was.

Then she was conscious of being close to him, but it was difficult to read his thoughts or be certain whether he was as acutely aware of her vibrations as she was of his.

'He is so strong, so dominating, so masculine,' she told herself, 'that no-one could meet him and think about anything else.'

When he put the ring on her finger she felt herself tremble.

She imagined it was because she was still afraid of having a husband just in case, even after what the *Duc* had said, she tempted him as her mother had tempted her father.

The Nuptial Mass was solemn and very moving in the centuries-old Chapel.

The servers were young boys from the village, and the Organist played music which made Ivona feel as if there were angels singing instead of a choir.

As the Priest blessed them, making the sign of the cross over their heads, she was very conscious that her mother was with her and praying for their happiness.

"I shall not be happy like you, Mama," Ivona wanted to say, "because the *Duc* does not love me, but I will do my best to be a good wife, and I know that I shall be safe with him and no longer menaced by Uncle Arthur."

Then as she prayed again that she might make the
Duc happy, she wondered if he was praying for her, or
perhaps thinking of somebody very different.

*   *   *

Now, as the train gathered speed, she was certain
that what he was praying for was peace, and that there
would be no confrontation with the Germans and no
loss of French lives if there was a conflict.

The *Duc* was very quiet, so she did not talk but
looked out the window.

As they travelled away from the snow-capped mountains down the valley with its silver river and the fir-
trees dark against the white fields, Ivona felt as if she
too was leaving something precious behind.

*   *   *

Later, they had a light but delicious meal served by
Gascoigne, who then retired to the small Pantry, intending to change to his own carriage at the next stop.

"I think perhaps it would be wise," Ivona said, "if I
went to bed."

"Yes, of course," the *Duc* agreed. "It has been an
exhausting day for you both mentally and physically."

"Did you mind being married so quietly," Ivona asked
impulsively, "without any of your friends there, and
without a large congregation?"

"It was how I have always wished to be married," the
Duc replied. "I think big, fashionable weddings are an
abomination."

Ivona smiled.

"I am glad. I thought perhaps I was depriving you of
something which you would regret in years to come."

"I hope neither of us will regret being married," the
Duc replied.

The note in his voice told her what he was thinking,
and after a moment she said:

"I am not frightened. . .but I should be very frightened indeed. . .if I had married. . .anybody but you."

"I can understand that," he replied, "but as you have

married me there is no reason to think about it any more."

"No, of course not," Ivona agreed.

She rose to her feet, a little unsteadily because the train was swaying, and the *Duc* rose too.

"I hope you have everything you want," he said. "If not, you have only to call me, as I am next door."

They walked into one of the two bedrooms which together took up half the coach.

Ivona's was slightly the larger, but they were both furnished with brass bedsteads and everything else was fitted neatly along the sides.

"I never thought I would find anything like this in a train!" Ivona exclaimed.

She remembered that sleeping-carriages in England were arranged in a very different way, although she had never slept in one.

"Actually, I designed this myself," the *Duc* said.

"You did? But how clever of you!"

She looked to where a basin was fitted against one wall, and against another was a chest-of-drawers which also constituted a dressing-table with a mirror above it.

"I shall be disappointed if you tell me I have omitted a great many things you need," the *Duc* said.

Ivona sat down on the bed.

"I am sure there will be nothing," she answered, "but because I think you are almost too perfect, I shall try to find some flaws!"

She was teasing him, and his eyes twinkled as he replied:

"I am certain that when we get to Paris you will find a great number, and if they are not obvious to you, there will always be plenty of 'kind' friends to point them out to you."

Ivona did not answer, and because the train was moving quickly the *Duc* sat down beside her on the bed.

"Perhaps I should have told you before, Ivona," he said, "that you looked very beautiful today as a bride, and I prayed, as I am sure you did, that our marriage would be a very happy one."

"Of course I prayed for that," Ivona replied, "and I shall try. . .very hard to make you a. . .good wife."

The *Duc* looked at her, then away, and she wondered what he was thinking.

Then on a sudden impulse she asked:

"If you were. . .tempting somebody. . .what would you . . . do?"

She thought the *Duc* looked surprised, and she said quickly:

"I am only curious because I could not expect you to offer a lady in whom you were interested an. . .apple."

The *Duc* laughed.

"I have an uncomfortable feeling that you are casting me in the role of the Devil!"

"No, no, of course not!" Ivona protested. "I am only discussing the subject entirely impersonally, because we spoke of it before."

"Of course," the *Duc* agreed, "and entirely impersonally shall I tell you that if I were tempting you as an attractive woman who was not my wife, I should want first to draw a picture of your face."

"I had no idea you were an artist!" Ivona exclaimed.

"Like an artist," the *Duc* replied, "I wish to engrave what I find beautiful on my memory, and this is how I should do it."

He leant forward as he spoke and with his first finger touched Ivona lightly on the side of her cheek just where it joined her hair.

"First," he said, "I should draw an outline of your face, which is very unusual and will, I am quite sure, be the delight of many portrait-painters before you are very much older."

As he spoke he drew his finger up along the top of her oval forehead and down the other side over her cheek and along her chin-bone.

It gave Ivona a strange feeling. At first it tickled her, then it was as if there were a little flame running over her skin.

"Having drawn the outline of your face," the *Duc* went on quietly, "I would then fill it in, starting with your adorable winged eye-brows."

He touched one after the other with his finger, then went on:.

"Then your small, straight nose."

As he spoke he ran his finger down her nose and into the dip of her upper lip.

Ivona was not certain why, but it made her draw in her breath.

The *Duc* paused before he said:

"I might find your lips a little difficult."

"W-why?"

It was hard to ask the question.

"Because they are very young, and have not yet been kissed."

"Does that. . .make them any. . .different?" Ivona whispered.

"One day you will know the answer to that," the *Duc* replied.

His fingers moved over her upper lip, then her lower one, and now she definitely felt as if there were fire on his fingers, and it aroused a very strange sensation in her breast.

The *Duc* unexpectedly rose to his feet.

"My portrait is finished for the moment, Ivona," he said. "Sleep well!"

Before she could reply, before she could say that she wanted him to stay and go on talking to her, he had left.

He shut the door of her room and she knew he had gone back into the Drawing-Room.

She sat very still, conscious that where his fingers had touched her eye-brows, her nose, and her lips, they were all throbbing.

'It is very strange,' she thought.

But she could not explain why it should be so.

It was a long time before she undressed and got into bed.

An hour later she heard the *Duc* going into the room

next to hers and wanted to call out to him to come to
say good-night.

But she thought he would not wish to be bothered
with her, and she wondered if perhaps he had thought
it immoral of her, or at least immodest, to ask him how
he tempted women.

But why touching her in such a way should be a
temptation she was not quite certain. She only knew it
gave her a strange sensation in her breasts.

When she fell asleep she could still feel his finger on
her lips.

*   *   *

When the train arrived in Paris early, there was a
carriage drawn by four horses waiting to take them to
the *Duc*'s house in the Champs Élysées.

Ivona realised how well organised everything was.

An enormous number of servants were waiting to see
to the luggage and to carry even their smallest possessions.

The Station Master escorted them from the train out
of the Station to where the carriage was waiting.

Ivona had only been in Paris once before, when she
had been with her mother and father to her grandfather's
funeral.

She had found entrancing the tall grey houses with
their shutters, and the cafés where even at this early
hour there were a number of people sitting outside
drinking aperitifs.

There were trees in every road already showing the
first tender green leaves of spring.

"We have left the snow behind," the *Duc* said with a
smile, reading her thoughts, as he did so often, "and
May in Paris can be very attractive."

"How long shall we be staying?"

"I am not certain," he answered, "but unfortunately
not for very long."

"I am. . .afraid of going to. . .England," she murmured.

"Not with me?"

"No, of course not. It will be perfectly all right if I

am. . .with you," she said a little uncertainly. "But. . .
supposing neither of us is. . .happy there?"

The *Duc* smiled.

"In which case we will go somewhere else. The world
is a big place and we can afford to travel, which is
something I, at any rate, intend to do."

"That will be wonderful!" Ivona cried, then added:

"Perhaps you will find it. . .boring if we are. . .alone
too. . .much!"

"When I do, I will tell you so," the *Duc* said. "After
all, it is important that we should be frank with each
other."

"Yes, of course," Ivona agreed. "And I will try not to
whine and complain, which the *Comte* always said he
found very irritating in a woman, and which my mother
never did."

"I am quite certain that if you are not pleased with
what is happening," the *Duc* replied, "you will flash fire
at me with your eyes, and doubtless will be extremely
outspoken on the subject."

"Why should you think I would be like that?" Ivona
asked.

"I think that would be much more characteristic of
you than to be subservient and ineffectual."

She was not certain whether this was a compliment
or not, but she answered:

"I am sure I should never wish to 'flash fire at you
with my eyes,' as you call it."

As she spoke she remembered the strange impression of fire which she had felt from the *Duc*'s finger and
wondered if that was what he was expecting from her
eyes rather than anger.

When they arrived at his house in the Champs Élysées,
it was just as impressive as Ivona had anticipated it
would be.

Again there were paintings, statues, and objets d'art
which made it seem like an Aladdin's cave.

She went from one treasure to another, exclaiming
over them and finding a collection of jewelled snuff-
boxes particularly entrancing.

"How can you possess all these beautiful things?" she asked.

"They are mine, and I intend to keep them so that when I am dead they can be passed on to my children and my grandchildren," the *Duc* said.

There was a harsh note in his voice which made Ivona aware that he was thinking they might be taken away from him by the Germans.

She was just about to say she was sure that he would be able to keep them safe, when it struck her that married as they were, they might never have children.

Ivona was very innocent because her mother had never talked to her of such things, but she knew that when people were married and made love to each other they had a baby.

For the first time she wondered if that was what the *Duc* wanted from her.

He had never said so, and she felt it was not anything she could discuss with him, however often he might say they must be frank with each other.

Then as if, once more, he knew what she was thinking, he said:

"I am sure that like me, Ivona, you believe in the continuity of a great family, and that the treasures that are passed down from previous generations are to be passed on to the next and not lost or squandered."

As he finished speaking, the *Duc* went from the room and Ivona stared after him in perplexity.

Was he, she wondered, telling her that he wanted her to be his wife completely and not only in name?

If so, surely he could make it a little clearer, and perhaps kiss her.

She remembered the feeling she had had when the *Duc*'s finger had touched her lips, and found herself wondering what it would be like if it had been his lips on hers.

She drew in her breath and again there was that strange little sensation within her breast for which she could not find a name.

Then as she stood there alone in the Salon, wondering and thinking about the magnificent but rather strange man who was her husband, she knew that she wanted him to kiss her.

* * *

The *Duc* insisted that Ivona should rest during the afternoon.

"I am not tired," she protested, "and there is so much to see!"

"There will be plenty of time for you to see all Paris later," he said. "I do not want you to be tired because I thought it might amuse you to dine out this evening."

Ivona's eyes lit up.

"In a Restaurant? The *Comte* always told Mama that aristocrats did not take their wives to Restaurants."

"This one is different," the *Duc* explained, "and I think it might amuse you. I want you to see it before we leave Paris. It is called the Café Anglais, but it is of course very, very French!"

Ivona laughed. Then she said:

"I would very much like to go into a Restaurant. I have never been in one, except for the little *estaminets* when we have been out riding all the day and not been able to get home until late."

"I will take you to the Café Anglais," the *Duc* said, "because it is the most distinguished of all the Restaurants in Paris, and anybody with any gastronomic pretensions feels obliged to go there as soon as they arrive."

"It sounds very exciting!"

"It is also filled with all the smartest and most important people in the Social World. So wear your prettiest gown, and tomorrow I intend to take you to Frederick Worth's to buy you a great many more."

Ivona gave a little cry of excitement.

Although she lay down as the *Duc* had ordered her to do, she found it difficult to sleep.

She had been very happy alone with her mother and the *Comte* in Alsace, but she had sometimes longed to have a peep at the world which he described so vividly but from which they were barred.

Now that was changed, and when she was dressed for dinner, with the help of what she was aware was a very experienced maid, the *Duc* came into her room holding a box in his hand.

When the maid had curtseyed and left, he said:

"Let me see what you are wearing for this very auspicious occasion."

She held out her arms, then twirled round to let him see the very large bustle that billowed out behind her.

It was a gown made from the very softest pink tulle and ornamented, as were all Worth's gowns, with flowers, ribbons, and diamante.

In this case the flowers matched the gown, while the ribbons were of a very pale blue and sparkled as if they had been sprinkled with rain-drops.

There were the same flowers on the low décolletage, and as Ivona looked at the *Duc* to see if he approved, he said:

"Very suitable! And I think what I have for you here will enhance even more the glamour of your appearance."

He opened the box he held in his hand as he spoke, and Ivona saw that it contained a diamond necklace of exquisitely worked flowers.

There were also earrings to match, and two bracelets.

"Are those for me?" she gasped.

"I bought them for you this afternoon," the *Duc* answered, "as my wedding-present."

"How can you give me anything so marvellous?"

"Let me put them on for you."

The *Duc* clasped the necklace round her neck, hung the ear-rings in the small lobes of her ears, then fastened the bracelets on each of her wrists.

"Now I feel like the Fairy Queen!" Ivona exclaimed.

"I have one more present," the *Duc* said, "for the *Duchesse* de Sancerre."

"Another?"

He drew a small ring-box from his coat and as he opened it she saw it contained a large heart-shaped diamond surround by smaller ones.

"Our engagement was very short," the *Duc* explained, "but I do not think you should be deprived of a ring."

"It twinkles like a star in the sky," Ivona said, "and like the moon that helped me to find my way to you."

"Which is something I hope you will never regret," he said quietly.

He put the ring on her finger, lifted her hand to his lips, and kissed it.

As he did so, Ivona felt as if a little shaft of moonlight ran through her body, or it might have been part of the fire she had felt before when he touched her.

"How. . .can I thank. . .you?" she asked.

"I do not want thanks."

"But I have to tell you how. . .grateful I am, and how. . .kind you are to. . .me."

"That is what I want to be," he said very quietly.

Then once again in the abrupt way he had done before he walked from the room, saying as he reached the door:

"I will wait for you downstairs. Do not be long."

Wearing a velvet stole trimmed with sable over her evening-gown, Ivona joined the *Duc* in the Hall.

Once they had set out in the carriage drawn by two horses down the Champs Élysées, she impulsively slipped her hand into the *Duc*'s.

"It is very exciting," she said, "going out like this with you."

His fingers closed over hers.

"I hope you will always think so," he said, "although of course the day may come when you may prefer another escort."

"That will never happen. . ." Ivona said, There was a little pause before she added: ". . .to me!"

The *Duc* said nothing, but she was thinking that he would want other women rather than herself, and then she would sit at home.

She told herself she was being unduly pessimistic, and yet what she had thought in the carriage was confirmed when they reached the Café Anglais.

The *Duc* seemed to know everybody in the Restaurant.

While the men greeted him enthusiastically, the women smiled at him from under their eye-lashes and held out their hands with extravagant gestures, as if they gave him their hearts.

But when the *Duc* introduced Ivona as his wife, his friends at first started as if they could hardly believe their ears, then stared at her with a curiosity that was embarrassing.

"You are married, Jules?" the *Duc*'s friends exclaimed. "Why were we not told, and why were we not invited?"

The *Duc* did not answer their questions, he only explained to Ivona who each of his men-friends was, extolling their possessions, their successes on the race-course, or their importance in politics.

Of the women there was nothing to say except that Ivona found each one more beautiful than the last.

One particularly beautiful woman exclaimed when she saw him:

"Jules! I had no idea you were back! How can you be so cruel as to reach Paris without telling me you were coming? I have missed you. *Mon Dieu!* How I have missed you!"

"I am gratified," the *Duc* said quietly, "and may I present you to my wife."

For a moment there was an astonished silence. Then the lady to whom he was speaking went so pale that Ivona thought she was about to faint.

Then she said in a voice that sounded strangled:

"Your—wife?"

"I am married," the *Duc* said, "and I feel sure you will be kind enough to congratulate me."

The woman facing him drew in her breath. Then she said:

"I would find it hard, Jules, to wish you anything but regrets!"

With that she turned on her heel and walked away, leaving the man who was accompanying her to congratulate the *Duc* in an embarrassed manner before he followed her.

When at last they were able to sit down at their

table, which Ivona realised was situated in the best position in the room, she said:

"I can see that by getting married you have upset quite a number of people!"

"They will get used to the idea," the *Duc* said lightly, "and I hope you noticed, once they had looked at you, how very sincere were the congratulations of my men-friends."

"Your lady-friends had a very different feeling!" Ivona said mischievously.

Then as the *Duc* started to order dinner and she looked round the Restaurant, she wondered how long it would be before he would be here with one of the lovely ladies who so obviously craved his attention.

In fact, they looked at him in such an admiring manner that Ivona felt it was somehow uncomfortable.

Then she remembered how the *Duc* had said that he was the tempter, not the tempted, the hunter, not the hunted.

She wondered if it really bored him when women pursued him, as those to whom he had just spoken were obviously eager to do.

The *Duc*, having given the order for wine, said:

"Now we can talk. Tell me what you want to know."

"Tell me about your friends, and why they are important enough to be in that category."

The *Duc* laughed.

"They would hardly think of themselves in that way."

"It is quite obvious that they admire you and, I expect, envy you."

"That is inevitable if a man is rich."

"I do not think it is a question of money," Ivona replied, "but rather because you are everything a man would want to be."

She was speaking seriously as she thought it out and did not notice the look the *Duc* gave her before he said:

"You will make me conceited, Ivona!"

"I doubt it. Mama always said conceited people were those who had nothing to be conceited about! It is not

conceit to be proud, to know one is right, or to be
aware that one can really excel in one particular field."

"I have never heard it explained quite like that
before," the *Duc* said, "and I find it one of the many
interesting things you have said to me."

"Do I really say interesting things?" Ivona asked. "I
am so afraid when you are so clever and so knowledgeable that you must find me very. . .boring."

"So far you have not bored me," the *Duc* assured
her. "In fact you have intrigued me, interested me, and
got me involved in your problems, so that I felt I had to
solve them."

"Were they a challenge?"

"Yes."

"Is that why you. . .married me?"

There was silence, and she thought the *Duc* was
thinking out his reply.

She looked at him, wondering what his reply would
be, when suddenly she was aware that there was somebody standing at their table.

She looked up and gave a startled gasp.

Her uncle was there, and there was an expression of
triumph on his face.

"So here you are!" he said in an accusing tone.

Ivona felt as if the walls of the room were crumbling
about her, and as she gave another gasp of fear, the
Duc put out his hand and laid it on her arm.

"Now that I have found you," the Marquis said harshly,
"you will come with me immediately! If you refuse, I
will fetch the Police!"

"That is where you are mistaken," the *Duc* said coldly.
"You are not at the moment, My Lord, speaking to
your Ward, but to my wife, the *Duchesse* de Sancerre,
over whom you have no legal jurisdiction."

The *Duc* spoke quietly and clearly, and for the moment the Marquis stared at him as if he could not
believe what he had said.

Then he repeatd:

"Your wife? Are you telling me that you have married
this felon?"

"We are married!" the *Duc* replied. "And now, since we are eager to enjoy our dinner, My Lord, I suggest that you leave us, and tomorrow morning, if you have any more to say on this matter, you can send your Solicitors to call on me."

As the *Duc* was speaking, the Marquis had gone crimson in the face, his eyes had darkened, and his thin lips had set in a hard line.

Then he said furiously:

"If you think you can cheat me in such a way, you are very much mistaken. I knew that you were lying to me, and that is why I have been having your house watched. You are a cheat and a bounder, and I very much doubt if any ceremony my niece has gone through with you is valid."

"You insult me!" the *Duc* replied, without raising his voice.

"That is what I mean to do," the Marquis answered, "and I repeat, you have cheated me by marrying my niece, as you doubtless cheat to make your horses win on the race-course!"

There was a silence so explosive that Ivona could only reach out and cover the *Duc*'s hand with hers.

She felt as if she were touching steel, as the *Duc* said slowly:

"I imagine, My Lord, you have some reason for insulting me in such a manner. I can therefore only request that you meet me in the honourable manner—if you know the meaning of the word—tomorrow morning."

It took Ivona a fleeting second to understand what he was saying. Then she exclaimed beneath her breath:

"No! No!"

"I will fight you and kill you!" the Marquis said, almost spitting the words.

"That remains to be seen," the *Duc* replied, "and as I imagine you wish such dramatics to be private, we will meet on the Bowling-Green of my house at six o'clock."

"I shall look forward to ending my association with you!" the Marquis retorted.

He looked at Ivona and added in a tone of venom:

"Enjoy yourself this evening, in your usual outrageous way, Ivona, for after tomorrow you will receive your just deserts!"

With that he turned and walked away from the table. Ivona saw him join her aunt at the end of the room, and they left the Restaurant together.

She was still shaking from shock and her fingers had tightened on the *Duc's* hand until her nails had cut into his skin.

Then as he beckoned the waiter to fill up their glasses with wine, she said in a voice he could barely hear:

"Can Uncle Arthur. . .really mean to. . .kill you?"

"He will try," the *Duc* replied, "but do not perturb yourself. He will not succeed."

Ivona remembered that the *Comte* had said that the *Duc* was a crack shot and most men were too afraid to challenge him, even if they felt they wanted to.

Then as she thought about it, she also remembered that her uncle had never cared for shooting, as her father had.

As far back as she could remember he had never shown any interest in the excellent game-shooting there was on his father's Estate in Bedfordshire.

"He must be. . .mad," she said, "to challenge. . .you in. . .such a way!"

"Let us forget about it," the *Duc* answered. "We are going to enjoy our first dinner in a Restaurant together, Ivona, and I see no reason why you should be upset by your uncle, who, as you say, is undoubtedly mad!"

"I am sure he has. . .grown like. . .Papa."

The *Duc* was not listening.

He was talking to her, as she had asked him to do, about the people in the Restaurant.

Although at first she found it hard to concentrate because her heart was pounding from the confrontation she had witnessed and her hands felt very cold, she gradually relaxed.

*   *   *

Later, when they had driven home and she was in bed, she thought that the only explanation for her uncle's behaviour must be that he really had become deranged.

Either that, or else he had no idea that the *Duc*, just as he was famous in so many sporting fields, also excelled in duelling and he had no chance of competing with him.

As they reached the *Duc's* house in the Champs Élysées and went upstairs, he said:

"Try to sleep now, Ivona, and I beg of you, do not worry about what will happen tomorrow morning. I promise I can look after myself."

He smiled before he added:

"You would think I was boasting if I told you how many duels I had fought in my life, and I have never yet been the loser."

"I. . .I am sure Uncle Arthur will fight you. . .unfairly!"

"I doubt it," the *Duc* answered. "After all, he is an English gentleman, and also a Parson. There must be something in his code that prohibits cheating!"

"All the same. . .I am frightened for. . .you!" Ivona said as they stopped outside her bedroom.

"Trust me, as you have trusted me in other things."

He looked at her and said:

"I wanted this to be a very happy evening for you. As your uncle has spoilt it, I will take you out again tomorrow evening to make up for it."

"I. . .would like that."

She held out her hand and saw the flash from her ring.

"And thank you for your wonderful presents," she added.

"They become you," the *Duc* answered, "but I have never yet seen you in anything in which you did not look lovely, except of course those extremely immodest trousers!"

Ivona laughed as he intended her to do, and he kissed her hand before he said:

"Good-night, and do not lose an hour's sleep over your abominable uncle. I will deal with him!"

He walked into his room, which was next to hers and joined by a communicating-door.

Her maid was waiting for her, and only when she had undressed and was in bed did she wonder if she could go into the *Duc's* room and talk to him.

She wanted him to reassure her that everything would be all right. She wanted to be quite certain that her uncle would not harm him.

Then she asked herself how that was possible.

She remembered a conversation that had taken place a long time ago when she was quite small and she had heard her father say:

"Arthur is opposed to my prosecuting a poacher whom the game-keepers have caught in one of the woods."

"Opposed?" her mother had enquired.

"He says I have no right to have the man imprisoned or transported for what he was doing."

"It does seem rather a harsh punishment," her mother had said softly.

"I have to protect what is mine," her father had said, "but Arthur does not understand. He is interested only in preserving birds, not in shooting them, which is not really surprising, considering he is such a bad shot!"

"Such a bad shot!"

Ivona repeated the words to herself.

Then why, knowing that he was a bad shot, did her uncle challenge one of the most outstanding marksmen in the whole of France?

He must be aware of the *Duc's* reputation, and if not, there would be plenty of people to tell him.

Thinking back over the scene in the Restaurant, she was certain that her uncle had made up his mind to force the *Duc* into a duel with him.

But why? Why? Unless he was quite certain he could kill him.

Because her anxiety made her feel so agitated, Ivona got out of bed and moved restlessly about her room, trying to guess what her uncle was planning.

She could see the jewellery the *Duc* had given her

glittering on the dressing-table where she had left it when she took it off.

Even as she looked at it she remembered that in her mother's jewel-box, which she had brought with her from the Château, there was something else besides jewels.

She picked up the box, found the key, and opened it.

The jewellery given to her mother by the *Comte* lay glittering on the velvet-lined tray.

She lifted up the tray, and while underneath there were more jewels, there was also in the bottom of the case something larger wrapped in chamois leather.

She drew out from it a small pistol.

The *Comte* had brought it to her from Paris soon after they had arrived in Alsace.

"Because I hate you being alone here so much, my darling," he had said, "even with the servants to defend you against intruders, I feel you should also be able to defend yourself."

Her mother had looked at the pistol he held out to her with its small handle decorated with amethysts, and laughed.

"A very attractive weapon!" she said. "As a matter of fact, I can shoot quite well."

"You can?" the *Comte* asked in surprise.

"My father taught me at the same time as he taught my brothers, because I was jealous that they should have so much of his attention."

"Come and show me how good you are."

The *Comte* had arranged a target in the garden, and after her mother had fired at it he kissed her and said:

"Now, if you sleep with that under your pillow, I shall not feel so worried about you as I have been these last few weeks."

"I want to shoot too!" Ivona had exclaimed.

"And so you shall!" the *Comte* answered. "But I am sure when you are grown up you will be so pretty that there will always be plenty of men ready and willing to protect you."

"You are not to say such things to her!" her mother interposed.

"Why not?" the *Comte* asked. "No pretty girl should be so stupid as not to realise she is pretty."

They both had laughed, and he had taught Ivona how to shoot with the pistol.

She had not been satisfied until she could hit the bull's-eye nine times out of ten.

Now, holding the pistol in her hand, she thought it was fate that she should have it with her and available at this particular moment.

She knew, with a conviction which no argument of the *Duc's* could break, that her uncle was up to some trick.

He may have genuinely believed that the *Duc* had cheated him, and so felt justified in cheating him in return.

"I must watch this duel!" Ivona decided suddenly.

It was something she instinctively shrank from, and it had not even entered her head until now to do so.

The *Vicomte* had arrived in the Restaurant as they were drinking their coffee and was surprised to see them.

"I had intended to call on you tomorrow morning, *Duchesse*," he said to Ivona, which made her aware that the *Duc* had already told him they were married.

"Call on me," the *Duc* said, "make it five-thirty."

"Five-thirty!" the *Vicomte* exclaimed.

"Come to the house, for we have an appointment in the usual place at the usual hour."

"I do not believe it!" the *Vicomte* exclaimed. "Who is your opponent?"

"Ivona's uncle!"

The *Vicomte* looked worried.

"You must be careful, Jules," he said. "I have been making enquiries about Morecombe, and he has been declaiming against you in the Travellers' Club in such a way that one or two of your friends have told me he must be insane!"

"That is exactly what Ivona and I both think," the

Duc said. "Nevertheless, after the way he insulted me this evening, I have to meet him! I want you as one of my seconds, and ask Henri if he will be the other."

"I know he will," the *Vicomte* replied, "and Dupré had better be the Referee as usual."

"Of course," the *Duc* agreed. "We can rely on him to be strictly fair, and also to get us out of any legal difficulties, if there are any."

"I will see to it," the *Vicomte* said.

When he left them, the *Duc* said to Ivona:

"You see, I will be in good hands."

"Yes. . .of course," she agreed.

Now she was quite certain that neither the *Duc* nor the *Vicomte* nor any of his friends realised how strangely out-of-character her uncle was behaving.

Always in the past he had been sanctimonious about anything that was not strictly within his very narrow Christian creed.

Why then should he suddenly wish to fight a duel, which was forbidden in France, although in fact they often took place?

In the past he had decried duels as being wicked and only indulged in by foreigners.

"There is something wrong. . .very wrong!" Ivona told herself.

When she went back to bed she put the pistol down beside her, and it was somehow comforting to know that it was there.

She was determined that whatever happened, she would make it her business to protect the *Duc* just in case he could not take care of himself as well as he thought he could.

"I cannot lose him," she said aloud.

Then she wondered why it mattered so desperately and why she was trembling. But she dared not answer her own questions.

Chapter Seven

Ivona crept silently down a side-staircase, finding her way by holding on to the bannister.

The curtains were still drawn and the house was very quiet.

She knew it was important that the *Duc* should not have the slightest idea that she was finding her way to the Bowling-Green.

If he saw her, she was certain he would send her back and forbid her to watch the duel, which she knew was considered very incorrect for a lady to do, and tell her not to fuss.

"Men hate being fussed at by women," her mother had always said.

Ivona knew the *Duc* felt so confident of winning that it would only irritate him if he thought she was worrying unduly.

The more she thought about it, the more she was quite certain that there was something very strange about her uncle's deliberate action in challenging him.

She found a door which led into the garden, thereby

avoiding the front of the house, where the servants, early though it was, might be moving about.

There were two bolts on it, which she pulled back with difficulty, but the key was in the lock and when she turned it she found it was well oiled.

Outside, the last stars were fading from the sky and there was a faint glow in the East which she knew from the books she had read would turn the grey roofs of Paris to silver.

All she could see, however, were trees, and the *Duc*'s garden, although not large, was well stocked with them. As many of them were chestnuts, she knew that in a week or so the buds would burst and they would glow like lighted candles on a Christmas tree.

Now everything was the soft green of spring and she felt as if she should be happy and carefree instead of consumed by a terror which seemed to seep through her veins like poison.

The garden immediately round the house was laid out in the traditional French manner in an intricate pattern with clipped box-hedges round a very beautiful stone fountain with a replica of Cupid in the centre.

She kept to the shrubs at the side of the formal garden so as not to be seen, and hoped that the shadows under the trees concealed her.

She walked on until she came to the Bowling-Green.

It was obvious that the long stretch of green lawn, as smooth as velvet and surrounded by flowers and shrubs, was a perfect place for a duel.

The blossoms scented the air, and the trees beyond them constituted a screen through which it would be impossible for any unauthorized person to observe what was happening.

Ivona crossed the green and walked into the shrubs on the other side to find they were high enough to conceal her even when she was standing.

She realised she would have a long wait and thought that later she would move to a better vantage point to watch what was happening.

In the meantime, she sat down amongst the shrubs.

By twisting and turning her head a little she could see almost the whole length of the Green, and she wondered who would be the first person to appear.

She had an idea, although she was not sure, that it was always the Referee who arrived last.

Then she thought of the *Duc* and of how fortunate she had been in finding him, when without his assistance she might easily have been recaptured and taken forcefully back either to the Nun or to her uncle and from there to the Convent.

Then there would have been no escape, not even by death.

She was deep in her thoughts when she was aware of a movement, and bending down to look beneath the leaves of the shrubs in front of her, she saw there was a man standing in the centre of the Bowling-Green.

For a moment she could see only his legs.

Then by parting the leaves very carefully she could see that he was not one of the contestants but was dressed like a servant, and, to judge by the grey of his thinning hair, he was middle-aged.

He then turned round, and as he walked in the direction in which she was sitting, she gave a gasp.

She could see now, because he had pulled back the loose coat he wore to put his hands in his pockets, that he was wearing the waistcoat of her uncle's livery.

Moreover, she recognised him.

He was a man called Heaver, her uncle's man-servant, and Ivona had always thought him a surly, disagreeable individual.

She supposed he had come to look round on her uncle's behalf.

Then as she watched him walk past where she was hiding, reach the end of the Bowling-Green, and turn to look back, she suddenly remembered something.

Heaver was the poacher whom her father had intended to prosecute after he had caught him shooting the pheasants in one of the big woods on his Estate, but he had been dissuaded by her uncle.

Looking back, she recalled that it was then that her uncle had taken Heaver into his service.

The man had never left him, perhaps because he had been unable to do so, as her uncle had a hold over him.

Now as these thoughts were turning over in her mind, Ivona could hear her mother say to her father:

"Your brother has certainly made that man of his a 'Jack-of-all-Trades'! One day he is waiting at table, the next he is cleaning out the stables!"

"It will keep him out of mischief!" the Marquis had replied. "All I am concerned with is that he does not go shooting my pheasants again. He is too good a shot, for one thing, which is more than I can say of Arthur!"

Ivona remembered him laughing as he spoke, because, as she had always been aware, he had no particular liking for his brother.

Now, almost as if the words were written in front of her in letters of fire, she knew why Heaver was there.

It was Heaver who would kill the *Duc*!

But as the duel was considered an honourable exchange between gentlemen, there would be no cry of "Murder!" and her uncle would take the credit.

She saw the plot so clearly that her first instinct was to run back and tell the *Duc* what was being planned.

Then she knew that it was doubtful if he would believe her, and in any case he would insist on following the strict code of what was expected of a sportsman and therefore would not cancel the duel, but would meet the Marquis as arranged.

"I must. . .stop him! I cannot let him. . .die!" Ivona told herself.

Then as she thought of the *Duc* being shot down by Heaver and lying dead on the grass, she knew that she loved him.

It was not an ecstasy but an agony, like a thousand knives being plunged into her body.

They were so sharp and so poignant that she felt the physical pain of them and knew that this was like dying by her own hand because the man she loved was being cruelly and deceitfully murdered.

'I cannot let it. . .happen!' she thought frantically.

Then she remembered that in the little reticule she carried with her was the pistol with its jewelled handle which she had taken from her mother's jewel-box.

She had thought when she placed it in the satin bag that she would have to use it on her uncle if he tried to shoot the *Duc* before the Referee's count reached "ten."

That was what she had reasoned out in her mind he would be likely to do.

Although she knew he would certainly be accused of being unsporting and would be ostracised by every gentleman in France, the *Duc* would be dead.

Although she felt sure that this was her uncle's plan, she had thought that even so he might not be skilled enough to hit the *Duc* in the back, and if he did, it might not kill him.

Even so, she was determined that if he did behave in such an unsportsmanlike way, she would certainly shoot at him.

If she was quick enough she might force his shot to go wide and save the *Duc* from being wounded at all.

It was all so vague and depended so much on supposition that she had really not thought it out completely in her mind but was only desperately afraid that that was what would happen.

Now she knew without any doubt that Heaver would kill the *Duc*, and with the two men firing at each other it would appear that it was her uncle who had wounded his opponent fatally.

It was so terrifying that Ivona was shaking with fear and put her hands up to her face. As she did so, she began to pray:

"Help me, Mama. . .help me! I love him as you loved the *Comte* and I. . .cannot let him die!"

She felt as if her prayer winged up to the sky.

Then she felt as if there were a hand on her head and somebody was near her.

The impression was so strong that for the moment she supposed that somebody had come up beside her while her eyes were covered, and it might even have been the *Duc*.

Then she knew it was not a living hand that had touched her or a living body of which she was conscious.

It was her mother who was there beside her, and she no longer need be afraid.

"Help me, Mama, help me," she said again.

No longer was it a desperate cry of despair, but the murmur of a child who knows its mother will comfort and sustain it.

Then her mother was gone, but she had taken away with her some of the desperation that Ivona had been feeling.

Instead, as if her intelligence had taken over the conflict in her heart, she looked to see where Heaver was.

He was entering the bushes at the far end of the Bowling-Green exactly opposite, Ivona was sure, the point where he expected the *Duc* to turn on the count of "ten."

Moving very softly and stealthily so that she did not disturb the shrubs through which she passed, Ivona inched her way until she was opposite him.

When she stopped, she thought at first that he was not there.

Then she remembered that because he was a poacher and used to moving quietly and if possible invisibly, she must expect him to be using all his wiles at this moment.

After she had stared across the Bowling-Green for some minutes she saw the flutter of a leaf that was not caused by the wind, and she knew exactly where he was.

By now the sky had lightened and the receding stars were almost invisible.

The first glow of the sun was sweeping away the sable of the night and illuminating the tops of the trees.

It was then that Ivona found it hard to breathe as she saw her uncle come striding onto the Green, accompanied by two men.

As he spoke to the men with him he was smiling, and

she knew it was because he was so supremely sure of himself.

Just a few seconds after him came the *Duc*, accompanied by the *Vicomte* and another man who Ivona knew was the man he had referred to as Henri.

The *Duc*, Ivona thought, was looking even more magnificent than usual.

Almost as if it were a flag of defiance he was wearing a white shirt and white cravat, while her uncle, wore dark clothing.

It was a trick, Ivona knew, that an experienced duellist looked on with contempt.

Her uncle and the *Duc* acknowledged each other coldly and she noted that her uncle had deliberately moved to the end of the Green opposite to where Heaver was hidden.

The *Duc* appeared to accept his choice without comment and took the other end, where the *Vicomte* helped him remove his smart, tight-fitting coat.

In his long black trousers and white shirt he looked, Ivona thought, very masculine and at the same time very elegant.

It was not only the way he looked, but because even at a distance she felt the vibrations from him that made him different from any other man she had ever known, her love welled up inside her as if it were a flood-tide that she could not control.

It was a feeling she had never expected to experience and very different from anything she had anticipated.

The love that had existed between her mother and the *Comte* had always seemed to her to be soft, gentle, and comforting.

She realised that the *Comte* was always trying to make up to her mother for the unhappiness, the cruelty, and the fear she had suffered as the wife of the Marquis.

But what Ivona felt for the *Duc* was different.

It was like a flame flickering in her body.

She wanted to run to his side and tell him she could not lose him, and that if he died she must die too because he mattered to her far more than life.

"I love him!" she whispered beneath her breath. "If he does not love me, at least I can see him, talk to him, be near him. Even if I am hanged for killing Heaver, I will not let Uncle Arthur's diabolical plan succeed!"

The Referee, who was standing in the centre of the Bowling-Green, was now calling the opponents to him.

He spoke to them for a moment in a low voice.

Then they each took a pistol from the box he offered them, and after a short consultation the Referee stepped to one side while the *Duc* and the Marquis stood back to back.

It was then that Ivona tightened her grasp on the little pistol and looked across the Green at the shrubs opposite her.

There was no sign of Heaver, but she knew he was there, and she knew the exact moment when he would fire at the *Duc* and kill him.

"I must be just one second quicker," she told herself.

She was so frightened she would fail and be too late, or perhaps too early, that she felt for a moment as if the shrubs and the whole garden swam in front of her eyes.

Then she told herself that this was not the moment to weaken.

She had to save the *Duc,* and if she did not do so, she would see him lying dead in front of her as she had seen the bodies of her mother and the *Comte.*

Then there would be no-one left whom she loved, and her life would be over too.

"Help me. . .Mama. . .please. . .help me!" she prayed.

Then once again she felt in some strange manner that she was not alone.

"Three-four-five. . ." the Referee was intoning, and Ivona was aware that the *Duc* was coming closer and closer to her.

Now it was only a question of seconds.

". . .eight-nine. . ."

It was then that the leaves opposite her moved. She had one swift sight of the barrel of a pistol, and without waiting she fired.

Even as she did so, the Referee said:

". . .ten!"

The *Duc* turned, and one second after the explosion from Ivona's pistol, he fired.

At the sound of the first shot, the Marquis, at the other end of the Bowling-Green, had turned round to fire vaguely in the *Duc's* direction, making quite sure that he did not hit his target.

Because he was so confident that the *Duc* was already mortally wounded, he did not keep himself in the prescribed duelling manner, sideways to his opponent, shooting across his left shoulder.

Instead, he faced the *Duc*, waiting triumphantly to see him fall to the ground.

The result was that the *Duc's* shot, aimed accurately and correctly at his left arm, hit him in the chest immediately above his heart.

As the Marquis staggered and fell backward onto the ground, Heaver's body collapsed in the shrubs in which he had been hiding, his right arm with the pistol in its hand protruding forward into view.

Ivona did not wait to see her uncle fall.

She knew only that the *Duc* was standing unhurt in front of her, and bursting through the bushes, with the twigs catching at her gown, she ran toward him.

Without thinking, driven only by her emotional relief that he was not dead, she flung herself against him.

"He meant to. . .kill you. . .he meant to kill. . .you!"

She held on to him, her arms round him, the tears running heedlessly down her cheeks.

The *Duc* looked first in bewilderment at Ivona, then at the arm of the man still holding the pistol whom he could see a few feet away from him.

Finally he looked at the prostrate body of the Marquis at the other end of the Bowling-Green, over which his seconds were bending.

"He was. . .waiting to. . .kill you!" Ivona whispered again.

The *Duc* looked at the pistol in her hand as if he could hardly believe what he saw. Then he took it from her.

As he did so, with his other arm he held her against him and said:

"Go back to the house, Ivona! I will not have you involved in this mess!"

She looked up at him as if she must reassure herself that he was all right.

But she was unable to see anything except his silhouette against the sky, because her eyes were blinded by tears.

It was then that the *Vicomte* said quietly beside the *Duc*:

"There was a man hiding in the bushes who would have shot you just before you fired, Jules, if the *Duchesse* had not killed him first!"

"She must not be involved in this," the *Duc* said sharply.

"No, of course not," the *Vicomte* agreed.

"Do as I tell you, Ivona," the *Duc* said gently. "Go back to bed, and I will come to you as soon as I possibly can."

Because she could not think for herself, but knowing his words made sense, she moved a little uncertainly away from him.

Then the *Vicomte* took her arm and helped her to where there was a path which would lead her back to the house.

"You were magnificent!" he said.

Then he left her to find her way alone.

She walked through the formal garden, and although she was not certain how she found it, there was the door into the house in front of her, and it was open as she had left it.

She went up the stairs, and as she reached the landing she could hear curtains being pulled back and knew the servants were awake.

Because she had no wish to speak to anybody, she slipped quickly into her bedroom and shut the door.

She was half-afraid, although it was unlikely, that her maid would come to help her undress, so she quickly took off her gown, hung it up in the wardrobe from where she had taken it, and, putting on her nightgown, got into bed.

As she laid her head on the pillows she felt as if she had been encompassed by a mist that had now slipped away from her and she came back to reality.

She had killed a man! She had saved the *Duc*, and although she had not even looked at her uncle as she left the Bowling-Green, she was sure he was dead.

"It is over! I am free!" she told herself.

She knew it was the last thing she wanted to be.

She was indeed free from being immured in a Convent, and free of all her father's relatives, but perhaps because they were no longer a menace the *Duc* would no longer wish to protect her.

"He married me to help me," she told herself miserably, "but now that I need love rather than help, he too will feel. . .free."

But they would still be married.

Then as if in a dream Ivona could see the faces of the beautiful women who had laughed up at him, and fawned on him in the Café Anglais.

They had made it very obvious how much they wanted him, and in some instances how much he had meant already in their lives.

'That is where he. . .belongs,' she thought.

She knew how inexperienced and uninteresting she must appear to him.

But she knew that now she no longer constituted a challenge, no longer presented a problem which had intrigued him, and she would just be the encumbrance she had always been afraid of being.

"I love. . .him! I love. . .him!" she cried agonisingly. "But I shall never mean. . .anything to him, and perhaps I shall only see him on. . .formal occasions or when duty makes it. . .imperative that we should appear. . .together."

She remembered how the *Comte* had spent more and more time with her mother and less and less at home, and how he had grumbled and complained when there was a Ball, an Assembly, or a family celebration at which he had to be with his wife.

'That is how the *Duc* will treat me,' she thought, 'and I shall not even have his children to keep me company.'

Tears began to run down her cheeks, slow, agonising tears which came from her despair and seemed to freeze her body so that she shivered with the cold of it.

Without the *Duc* she knew she would be alone, utterly alone, and she thought perhaps it would have been better if she had died drinking the laudanum rather than giving it to the Nun.

Then once again she felt the knives of agony as she thought she must lose the *Duc*. He would not now be lying dead, but very much alive, but with. . .other people.

"Why did I not realise I loved him when I was hiding in his bed?" she asked.

Then she remembered how indifferent he had seemed at her being there.

It made her even more certain that he was not interested in her as a woman.

* * *

It must have been an hour or more before the communicating-door between their bedrooms opened and the *Duc* came in.

Now, because the sun was shining through the curtains, the room was filled with a golden glow and Ivona could see him clearly as he came toward her.

He had taken off the clothes in which he had duelled and was instead wearing a long dark robe which made him look taller than he actually was.

She stared up at him as he stopped by the bedside, and while her eyes seemed too big for her face, he could see the tears on her cheeks.

He sat down on the bed in front of her and said:

"You need no longer be afraid. Everything has been cleared up and your uncle has been taken to Hospital."

"He is. . .not dead?" Ivona asked in a whisper.

"Not yet," the *Duc* replied, "but the Surgeon said he

would die within the next hour or two, which makes everything easier from a legal point of view."

"And. . .Heaver?"

"If that was the name of the man who intended to kill me," the *Duc* replied, "you shot him brilliantly, Ivona. He died instantly and without pain."

Ivona drew in her breath.

"You saved my life," the *Duc* said very quietly.

"I was afraid. . .desperately afraid that he might. . .kill you before I could. . .kill him."

"But I am, as you see, alive, and very grateful, so we will not talk about it or even think of it."

Ivona did not speak. She was only thinking how much she loved the *Duc* and wondering if now he would say that their marriage had been quite unnecessary.

He drew a handkerchief from the pocket of his robe and, bending toward her, very gently wiped away the tears from her cheeks.

"No more tears," he said. "There is nothing left to frighten you. You are free!"

"B-but we are. . .still married."

"We are married," the *Duc* confirmed.

There was a little silence. Then he asked:

"Does that worry you? Would you rather it had not happened, now that your uncle can no longer be a menace?"

"I thought. . .perhaps. . .you would. . .regret it."

"I told you I wanted a wife."

"But not perhaps. . .like this."

He looked at her, but she did not understand the expression in his eyes. Then he said:

"Are you saying in a somewhat round-about manner that you wish to leave me?"

"No, no! Of. . .course. . .not!"

The words burst from Ivona's lips, and she said:

"But you may wish to be. . .rid of me. . .please. . . please let me stay with you. . .do not leave me. . .alone all the time. . .I want to be with. . .you!"

The words tumbled over themselves because she could

not think exactly how to say them or to explain what she was feeling.

"I have no intention of leaving you," the *Duc* said. "Have you forgotten? I have not yet finished my portrait of you."

It was not what she had expected him to say, and she looked up at him in surprise.

He put down the handkerchief with which he had wiped away her tears and cupped her small chin in his fingers.

That was something he had not done before, and once again she felt as if a little flame of fire ran over her skin.

She could also feel the strange sensations in her breasts, which grew and became more intense with his touch.

Then he bent forward and it flashed through her mind that he might kiss her, and her lips were ready and waiting for him.

Instead he moved his mouth very gently over her chin where he had just touched it, then, almost like a butterfly's kiss, he moved higher until his lips touched the corner of hers.

It was impossible to breathe, and she waited, feeling that if he did kiss her it would be the most wonderful thing that had ever happened.

Instead, he moved to the other side, and she could feel his lips, so gentle, so light, yet seeming to burn their way and to make the fire in her heart feel as if it must burst into flame.

Then as she felt herself tremble, but not with fear, the *Duc* raised his head to look down at her.

"You are so lovely!" he said, and his voice was deep.

She could not speak, she could only stare at him, feeling as if her whole body pulsated with sensations that were so strange, so bewildering, that it was impossible to think.

Then as very slowly his lips came nearer, the whole world was still and quiet and there was only him.

"So very lovely!" he repeated.

His lips were on hers and the fire in her breast seemed to explode. This was what she had been longing for, afraid of losing, and was life itself.

He kissed her until she could only feel as if he carried her into the very heart of the sun.

They were burning together with the wonder and glory of it, and it was so divine, so utterly perfect, that Ivona felt they must have died and this was Heaven.

* * *

A long time, a very long time later, Ivona turned her head against the *Duc's* shoulder and said in a little whisper:

"I. . .love you!"

She moved a little closer and felt his lips on her forehead as he replied:

"My precious, my darling little wife, I did not frighten you?"

"I thought we had both. . .died and were in. . .Heaven because it was so. . .perfect."

"That is what I wanted you to feel, and I meant to be very gentle, just in case your fears were still there."

"I could never be. . .afraid with. . .you."

"You were afraid of love and marriage."

"Now I am only. . .afraid that I may. . .bore you. . .and you will one day. . .leave me for all the beautiful women who. . .love you."

The *Duc* smiled.

"I knew you were thinking that, but, my darling, do you not understand that you are the woman I have been looking for all my life, and thought it impossible to find?"

There was a little silence before Ivona asked:

"Are you. . .really saying. . .that to me?"

"I have made love to many women," the *Duc* admitted, "but always my instinct, or what you and I call my 'voices,' told me that what I felt was not real love—the love I have for you—which is quite different, and which I could give only to somebody who is the other half of myself."

"Are you saying that is. . .me?"

"When you came into the hut," the *Duc* said, "I felt as if you brought the light with you."

"But you thought I was a boy."

"I did not think anything at the moment except that I was pleased to see you," the *Duc* replied. "Then when you knelt down by the fire I knew you were a woman, and special to me!"

"How could you have known that?"

"I cannot answer that question," he said, "but my 'voices' told me that you were very different, unique, something I must never lose."

Ivona put her arm across his chest as if to hold him to her.

"Why did I not feel that?"

"You are very young," the *Duc* replied, "and such instincts take a long time to develop."

She turned her face up to his.

"Teach me," she begged, "tell me how to be. . .like you."

The *Duc* laughed and it was a soft and tender sound.

"I want you to be like yourself, my lovely one, and that is quite enough for me."

"Why did you not tell me. . .before what you were. . . feeling?"

"Because I knew what *you* were feeling."

She gave a little sigh, and he said:

"I saw the fear in your eyes, and when you explained to me what had happened, I understood only too well how deeply it had affected you."

His hand moved over the softness of her body so that she quivered as he said:

"I wanted you more than I have ever wanted anybody in my whole life! But I was afraid of losing you."

"How could you have been. . .afraid of. . .that?"

"It was not entirely a physical feeling," the *Duc* went on, "but a mental and spiritual one."

His arm tightened round her as he said:

"I want you to belong to me completely and absolutely,

my precious, with every thought you think, with every breath you breathe!"

"That is how I do belong to you," Ivona said, "and when I thought you might. . .die, I knew that my life would. . .end too. I could not have gone on. . .living without. . .you."

"Now we are going to be together, and there are so many things for us to do—go to England, explore the world—and later, my darling, have a family."

He was watching her as he said the last words, and as she lifted her face to his and he saw the radiance in her eyes, he knew that the last fear had gone.

"I will give you lots and lots of sons," she said. "They will all ride as well as you do, shoot as well as you do, and be very nearly, although not quite, as magnificent as you are!"

The *Duc* laughed.

"I told you that you will make me conceited."

"You could never be anything but wonderful. . .marvellous. . .the kindest person in the whole world!"

Ivona's voice broke and there were tears in her eyes as she said:

"I am so wildly. . .ecstatically happy that I cannot believe I am not. . .dreaming!"

"You are awake," the *Duc* assured her, "and beginning a new life with me."

"That is all I want, and please, darling, marvellous, perfect *Monseigneur*, teach me so that I do not make mistakes. . .and most of all. . .do nothing that you would not. . .like."

"I love and adore everything about you," the *Duc* replied, and his voice was deep, "except, my precious darling, I will not allow you ever again to disguise yourself very ineffectively as a man."

Ivona gave a little chortling laugh.

"You need not be afraid of that! I want to be a woman. . .your woman. . .for you to admire me. . .and . . .love me."

Ivona spoke the last words a little shyly, and the *Duc* said:

"You are quite sure that is what you want?"

He turned round toward her as he spoke, so that she was lying beneath him.

He could feel her heart beating beneath the soft movement of her breasts, and because his body was touching hers, she was quivering.

There was no need for her to answer his question, for when he looked into her eyes he could see a little flickering flame that echoed the fire which he felt rising within himself.

He knew that as a woman Ivona excited him wildly, although he had never before in his life had to exert such self-control as he had these past days in doing nothing to frighten her.

He had been afraid of being too impetuous in making her aware of his love.

He had made her respond to him, or, as she would have said, he had tempted her.

Now while he knew how innocent and inexperienced she was, he also knew that spiritually they were perfectly attuned to each other, and he had never in his life been so attracted, so intrigued, so thrilled.

At the same time, he had a reverence for Ivona that was different from anything he had felt for any other woman.

He knew that she had captivated and enchanted him, and they were linked together by their instincts and by the spiritual awareness which was part of his "voices."

Because she was everything he wanted, the complement of himself, he was afraid that she might vanish and he would lose her.

"You are mine!" he said fiercely. "Mine, completely and forever!"

"I. . .love you! I love you. . .and love you. . .until there is nothing in the whole world. . .but you."

She put her hands flat on his chest and added:

"No, that is wrong! You are the world. . .the sky. . .the sea. . .and you are also the sun. . .the moon and the stars. . .there is nothing except you. . .and I worship you!"

As she spoke the last word, the *Duc's* lips were on hers.

Then as once again their bodies were joined, as were their minds and their hearts, the *Duc* lifted Ivona up onto the peaks of ecstasy.

The fire of their love gave them the rapture and glory of the Divine, which is boundless, since it comes from Eternity and goes on to Eternity.

There is no end to it, but for ever and always a beginning.

ABOUT THE AUTHOR

Barbara Cartland, the world's most famous romantic novelist, who is also an historian, playwright, lecturer, political speaker and television personality, has now written over 350 books and sold over 350 million books throughout the world.

She has also had many historical works published and has written four autobiographies as well as the biographies of her mother and that of her brother, Ronald Cartland, who was the first Member of Parliament to be killed in World War II. This book has a preface by Sir Winston Churchill and has just been republished with an introduction by Sir Arthur Bryant.

Love at the Helm, a novel written with the help and inspiration of the late Earl Mountbatten of Burma, Uncle of His Royal Highness Prince Philip, is being sold for the Mountbatten Memorial Trust.

In 1978, Miss Cartland sang an Album of Love Songs with the Royal Philharmonic Orchestra.

In 1976, by writing twenty-one books, she broke the world record and has continued for the following six years with 24, 20, 23, 24, 24, and 25. She is in the *Guinness Book of World Records* as currently the top-selling authoress in the world.

She is unique in that she was #1 and #2 in the Dalton List of BestSellers, and one week had four books in the top twenty.

In private life Barbara Cartland, who is a Dame of the Order of St. John of Jerusalem, Chairman of the St. John Council in Hertfordshire and Deputy President of the St. John Ambulance Brigade, has also fought for better conditions and salaries for midwives and nurses.

Barbara Cartland is deeply interested in vitamin therapy and is President of the British National Association for Health. Her book, *The Magic of Honey*, has sold throughout the world and is translated into many languages.

Her designs, *Decorating with Love*, are being sold all over the USA and the National Home Fashions League made her "Woman of Achievement" in 1981.

Barbara Cartland Romances (book of cartoons) has just been published in Great Britain and the United States, and several countries in Europe carry the strip cartoons of her novels.